ANNE
FRANK
and me

ANNE
FRANK
and me

by Cherie Bennett and Jeff Gottesfeld

G. P. PUTNAM'S SONS

NEW YORK

Library of Congress Cataloging-in-Publication Data

Bennett, Cherie. Anne Frank and me / by Cherie Bennett and Jeff Gottesfeld.

p. cm.

"Adapted from the play Anne Frank and me, Dramatic Pub. Co., 1997."

Summary: After suffering a concussion while on a class trip to a Holocaust exhibit,

Nicole finds herself living the life of a Jewish teenager in Paris during the Nazi occupation.

1. Holocaust, Jewish (1939–1945)—France—Paris—Juvenile fiction. [1. Holocaust, Jewish

(1939–1945)—France—Paris—Fiction. 2. Jews—France—Paris—Fiction. 3. Paris (France)—History—

1940–1944—Fiction. 4. France—History—German occupation, 1940–1945—Fiction.

5. Space and time—Fiction.] I. Title. II. Gottesfeld, Jeff.

PZ7.B43912   An 2001

[Fic]—dc21   00-055251   ISBN 0-399-23329-6

5 7 9 10 8 6 4

For Joseph Ozur, who lived, and for his family, who died;
for the Mullers and Gottesfelds who did not survive;
and in honor of the Righteous Gentiles.

ACKNOWLEDGMENTS

Above all, thank you to the Jewish community of Nashville, Tennessee; its Jewish Community Center commissioned our play and underwrote the world premiere. And to Professor Jacques Adler (*The Jews of Paris and the Final Solution,* New York: Oxford University Press, 1987), who has fact-checked and consulted on this project for years. Also to Anne Frank Center USA, Simon Wiesenthal Center, University of Judaism, YIVO Institute, the United States Holocaust Memorial Museum and the many French survivors to whom that institution introduced us. Also to Professors Deborah Lipstadt (*Denying the Holocaust,* New York: Free Press, 1993), Susan Zuccotti (*The Holocaust, the French, and the Jews,* New York: Basic Books, 1993), Joyce Apsel and Holli Levitsky; David and Suzanne Winton, Stanley Brechner, Jeff Church, Moses Goldberg, Rob Goodman, Bryan Cahen, Ed Finkelstein, Bruce Rogers, Rabbis Stephen Fuchs, David Davis, and Zalman Posner, John Lo Schiavo S.J., Revs. Joel Emerson and Ann Bassett, Claude and Mirella Luçon, Jack Pollak, the Windisch and Chanderot families, Kate Emburg, Bill Younglove, Sofya Weitz-Levitsky, Abby Lessem, Karen Pritzker Vlock, the Gottesfelds and Bermans, Josh Kane, Refna Wilkin, our editor Susan Kochan, Nancy Paulsen, Laura Peterson, and Dramatic Publishing Company. Thanks, too, to sister authors Jane Yolen, Lois Lowry, Han Nolan, Carol Matas, Miriam Bat-Ami, Edith Baer, Norma Fox Mazer, and Sonia Levitin, lights to the nations and to us. We are indebted to the scholarship of Adler, Lipstadt, Zuccotti, Jeremy Joseph, Georges Weller, Henri Amouroux, Michael Marrus and Robert Paxton, Melissa Muller, Claude Levy and Paul Tillard, and Serge and Beate Klarsfeld, among many others. References to Anne Frank's diary are from *The Diary of Anne Frank: The Critical Edition.* (New York: Doubleday, 1989).

Girl X website design and execution by Lindsay Hurteau, age 15, Granby, Massachusetts.

ANNE FRANK
and me

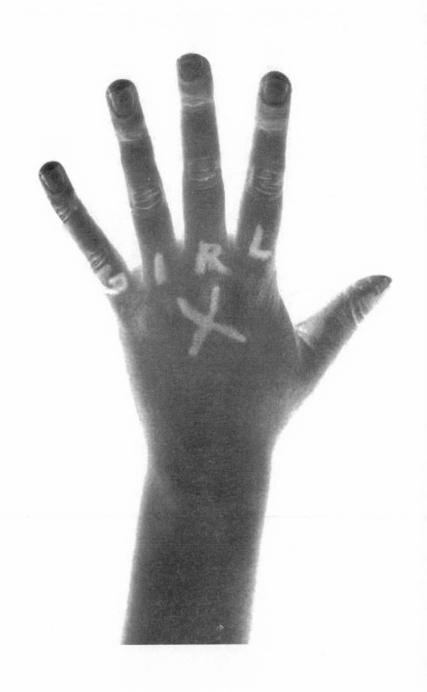

CAUTION!!! WEBSITE UNDER CONSTRUCTION!!!

Day 1, 8:20 p.m.

There are only four possible reasons you are reading this:

1. You know who Girl X is. But since that applies only to my best friend, M, that rules you out.

2. You're a perv surfing the Net who thinks the X in Girl X means X-rated. Wrong. Wipe off the drool, get a life, and surf on.

3. You're actually interested in the secrets of a tenth-grader in the burbs who is none of the following:
   a. smartest
   b. dumbest
   c. prettiest
   d. ugliest
   e. hippest
   f. geekiest

The only thing remotely interesting about me is that I can dance. Other than that, most of the time, I'm just *there*. Someday, at our twentieth class reunion, with cheesy blown-up yearbook photos on the walls and a low-rent cover band playing Puff Daddy from what you will refer to as "the best years of our lives," I'll be the one you don't remember.

Some People: Seem to be born knowing exactly who they are and where they're going; with a Day-Glo-highlighted road map to life.

Other People: Are Under Construction, Detours Ahead, mapless, figuring it out as they go.

I am one of the Other People. And the only reason I can think of for why you might still be reading this is:

4. You're just like me.

CAUTION!!! WEBSITE UNDER CONSTRUCTION!!!

Day 2, 9:15 p.m.

Frightening Thought du Jour: We are teen rodents of civilization, destined to run through a suburban maze at the end of which is the processed cheese: a life just as boring as our parents'.

Random Acts of Blindness: I am such a cliché. I am in love with J, a boy who does not seem to know I exist.

Confused Much? Today, a bad rep is a good thing. Everyone wants to be bad, badder, the baddest. Say you've had sex even if you haven't. Live Hip or Die.

Girl in the Middle: On one side of me, the sanctimonious Join-hands-at-the-flagpole-every-morning-because-True-Love-Waits kinda girls. On the other side of me, the pathetic Got-pregnant-on-purpose-kept-the-baby-who's-in-day-care-down-the-hallway-while-I-go-to-class kinda girls.

None of the Above: I am still among the (as M calls it) Have-not-yet-succumbed-to-the-Call-of-the-Wild. But why wait? I mean, what's the point, if it's the right guy? When's the "right time," anyhow?

Smokin': I fantasize about sex with J all the time; dream it when I'm asleep, daydream it when I'm awake. Makes me feel like I'm in free fall. What would it be like, really?

Girl X Manifesto: Live, love, feel everything, fear nothing, never settle, never regret, never die.

Caution!!! Website under construction!!!

Day 3, 10:09 p.m.

Girl Over the Top: Sometimes I am numb. Nothing matters. Other times, when I let myself feel, I feel too much. Bleed for everything.

They Say to Me: You will "outgrow" this and "grow up."
I Say to Them: What does that mean? To stop caring?

The Truth Hurts, So? There are some people meant for greatness. Then there are the rest of us. I'm not the stars or the sun—I don't radiate heat. Or the moon—I don't shine like a beacon to light the way. I am definitely not a celestial body. I'm an earthbound girl destined to revolve around someone else. And I would gladly revolve around J, who is the sun, the moon, and the stars put together. Loving him is a sickness. A fever.

Frightening Thoughts du Jour:
    a. I am obsessed.
    b. I hate that I feel this way.
    c. I have such disdain for girls like me.

000001 MAGIC COUNTER

one

Nicole Burns sat in the fourth row, third seat of Renee B. Zooms' English class, watching the door and at the same time pretending not to. An elderly woman entered, looking around uncertainly. Zooms greeted her warmly. Nicole's eyes slid back to the door. She was on alert for one thing. Him. J. Jack.

Her best friend, Mimi, flew in; loose-limbed skinny legs sliding into the seat across from her. Mimi had recently gone retro hippie; ratty bell-bottoms, COSMIC KARMA T, love beads. She leaned close, and patchouli scent wafted everywhere. "So, Nico. I checked out Girl X last night."

"I know, I saw a hit on my counter. My public confessional now has an audience of one. Remind me why I'm doing this again."

"You have a desperate need for attention?" Mimi ventured.

"It's anonymous."

"True. Maybe you have a deeply disturbed need to bare

the details of your secret, steamy existence to utter strangers."

Nicole dead-eyed her. "My life, as you know, is steam-free."

"Also true." Mimi shrugged. "So do what everyone else does. Lie."

"Meem, the whole point is to tell the truth, even if—"

Nicole's voice dropped off; her internal organs rearranged themselves. J had just walked in. Her eyes followed as he went to talk with his supposedly former girlfriend, Heather the Perfect.

Mimi peered at Nicole. "Amazing. I can actually see your IQ slump."

Nicole watched closely as Heather laughed and put one hand on Jack's right bicep. Then the bell rang shrilly; Jack and Heather took their seats.

"Settle down, people," Zooms said, the closing door underscoring her sentence. "One of the first assignments for your biennial Holocaust studies unit was to watch the adaptation of Jane Yolen's novel *The Devil's Arithmetic* on TV last night. Hands of those who did?"

A few hands hit the air: Mimi; the new girl, Suzanne Lee; a geek girl in the back row. Jack. David Berg. Not Nicole. She'd spent last night working on Girl X.

Pursuing invisibility, Nicole slunk down in her seat as her teacher smiled thinly. "Delightful. Five out of thirty-one. I could weep. Somehow the words *pop quiz* spring to mind. However, this is your lucky day. Instead of a pop quiz, we have a guest speaker. Feel free to thank her for your reprieve. It is an honor to introduce Mrs. Paulette Litzger-Gold."

The old woman that Nicole had seen enter the classroom stood to a smattering of grateful applause. "I thank Ms. Zooms for inviting me," she began, her voice slightly accented. "Why am I here to speak with you? Because I lived through the Holocaust. So, about me. I grew up in the most wonderful, sophisticated place in the world, Paris, France. What you do for fun now—go to movies, go shopping, listen to the latest music—is what my friends and I did then. In 1940, when I was your age, if someone had told me what was about to happen to me, I would not have believed it. But just five years later, I was liberated from a Nazi concentration camp more dead than alive."

The woman stopped for a sip of water and Nicole's eyes slid to Jack. From her seat behind him, Heather dropped a folded paper onto his desk. He read it, then turned around to grin at her. She smiled back. It was not the smile of a girl who was an *ex*-anything.

Mrs. Litzger-Gold went on with her story, about race laws and ration cards and resistance movements. Nicole was present in body only. Her mind was busy dealing with the Jack-Heather thing. Out of the corner of her eye, she saw Zooms staring daggers at her. She slapped a perky I'm-so-interested mask on her face.

"If you find the things I am telling you unimaginable, I understand," Mrs. Litzger-Gold was saying. "They seem unimaginable to me, too, even though I was there. Certain moments are burned into my memory. Such as the time French police knocked on the doors of Jewish homes in the dead of night. Many thousands were rounded up and taken to the Vélodrome d'Hiver, a sports arena that would become a temporary prison. There was no food nor water nor sanitary facilities. Some killed themselves because the world had turned into a place in which they no longer wanted to live. I remember Drancy, the detainment camp outside of Paris where so many were held and then deported. And I have not yet begun to tell you about the horror of the concentration camps, the SS, and the crematoria. I also remember the good—an apple given by a stranger, the underground press, some defiant words on a scrap of paper that gave me strength to go on."

Chrissy Gullet's hand sprang into the air.

"Miss Gullet, what burning question forces you to interrupt our speaker?" Zooms asked, her tone withering.

"I don't mind at all," the old woman insisted. "There are no bad questions, only bad answers. Please, young lady, go ahead."

Chrissy shook her hair off her face with a practiced gesture. "Okay, in fifth grade we read *Number the Stars*. We already know about the Holocaust. I'm very sorry that you had to go through it, but I don't understand why we have to talk about it again. I mean, we don't have Irish Famine Awareness Week, or How We Stole from the Native Americans Awareness Week, do we?"

From the next row, dark-eyed David Berg, smart, serious, intense, glared at her. "You are monumentally ignorant."

"Excuse me, David, but this is America, okay? Which means I'm entitled to have a different opinion from you."

"And I'm entitled to tell you what an idiot you are."

"Leave out the name-calling, Mr. Berg," Zooms warned. "Mrs. Litzger-Gold, would you like to continue?"

The old woman answered with a gesture that clearly invited the discussion to go on.

"Thank you," Chrissy told her. "Okay, David, no offense, but you're not really objective about this."

"Why, because I'm Jewish?"

Mimi turned to Chrissy. "Try to keep up. The Holocaust was international genocide."

"Yuh, I got it," Chrissy singsonged. "But it's not like it could ever happen here."

Zooms scanned their faces. "Could it? Today, in America, could it happen?"

"Yes," David answered. "Of course it could happen here."

Eddie Valley snorted out a laugh. "My man, Mr. Paranoid."

"I think it could happen here, too," Suzanne said mildly. Nicole smiled at her. Suzanne was pretty, nice, and had perfect strawberry blond hair. Three weeks before, Nicole had invited her to join her hip-hop trio.

"*Please.*" Chrissy punctuated this with an eye roll. "All I'm saying is, this is America in the twenty-first century, not

Europe a zillion years ago. No offense, ma'am, but the Holocaust is totally irrelevant ancient history."

Mrs. Litzger-Gold looked bemused. "Perhaps you are right about the history part, though I don't think of myself as ancient. But irrelevant? I cannot agree with you there."

Zooms swept her arms over the room. "Other opinions? People?" The usual suspects joined the debate. Jack was so impressive when he spoke—fair to both sides. He was just so *everything*. How could one guy be so—

"Miss Burns?"

Instant face flush, heart hurtling toward heaven. Zooms stared at Nicole. "Uh . . . sorry?"

"Eloquent as always, Miss Burns. I'll come back to you when you've gathered your thoughts." Zooms' laser-beam gaze fell on a guy in the back row. "Mr. Hayden?"

Nicole went limp with relief as all eyes went to Richard Hayden, a much bigger fish for Zooms to eviscerate. Eddie Valley had nicknamed him Dr. Doom for his habitual outfit: oversized army jacket, black shirt, and black pants. Dr. Doom got shortened to Doom, which is what everyone called him now.

"Your opinion, Mr. Hayden?" Zooms pressed, as Doom slumped in his seat, staring out the window. Weeks ago, he had announced that he'd no longer be taking part in classroom discussions. Zooms hadn't called on him since. Until now.

"Mr. Hayden, I asked you a question."

12

Silence.

"In the absence of a coherent response, might I assume that flunking my class is appealing to you?"

Doom remained mute, unreadable under Zooms' gaze. She refused to give in. Long seconds ticked by. Then, still staring out the window, Doom spoke. "My grade should be based on my test scores and the quality of my papers. Class participation is inane and entirely subjective."

Zooms stepped between Doom and the window. He neither looked at her nor looked away. "Did you listen at all to what our guest speaker said, Mr. Hayden? Would you agree that some things are worth speaking up for? Or against?"

Silence.

"I realize you are doing this to irritate me," she continued. "Congratulations on your success. Now, are we to assume that your silence means you agree with Adolf Hitler, that the world should be *Judenrein*—Jew-free?"

Slowly, Doom turned his head to look directly at Mrs. Litzger-Gold. Nicole shivered.

Zooms strode to the front of the room. "Hopefully, the rest of you can overcome your adolescent self-absorption long enough to recognize the importance of speaking out in the face of tyranny. And the paper you'll be writing on that subject—thanks to your colleague Mr. Hayden—will reflect that. A thousand words. Due next Thursday."

"Thanks, Doom," Eddie muttered. Someone else hissed "Freak" in Doom's direction.

Zooms checked her watch. "Unfortunately, the bell is about to ring. Now, I'm sure you'd like to thank Mrs. Litzger-Gold for speaking with us today." She led the class in applause, until the bell rang and kids flew from their seats as if shot from a catapult.

"Remember, people," Zooms called. "We meet in front of the school tomorrow morning at eight o'clock sharp for our field trip to the *Anne Frank in the World* exhibit. On Monday we'll discuss her diary and the exhibit. I suggest you anticipate a pop quiz."

A few kids stayed behind to talk with Mrs. Litzger-Gold. Nicole hung back because Jack had gone to ask the old woman a question. Then it hit her: This was her chance. All she had to do was to go up there and pretend she had a question, too. Jack would notice. He'd be impressed with her sensitivity. For the first time, he would really *see* her.

She headed for the front of the room, trying to come up with a question for the speaker. What happened to your family? That might be good. At that moment, Mrs. Litzger-Gold finished answering Jack and looked directly at Nicole. The weirdest feeling came over Nicole, as if she was somehow *connected* to this woman.

"Thank you again, ma'am," Jack said, as he walked away. For once, Nicole's eyes didn't follow him. They were still locked on the old woman's face.

"Have we . . . met before?" Nicole ventured.

"Have we?"

"Ironic question, Miss Burns," Zooms called. She was

closing the classroom windows. "Considering that you weren't listening when Mrs. Litzger-Gold was speaking."

Nicole's face burned. "I was listening." Her eyes went back to Mrs. Litzger-Gold. For some reason, Nicole didn't want to lie to her. "To tell you the truth," she said, her voice low, "I really wasn't listening to you much."

The old woman smiled. "To tell you the truth, I already knew that. I also know you stayed behind to talk to that handsome boy and not to me."

"You're right. I'm sorry."

Mrs. Litzger-Gold cocked her head to the side, still contemplating Nicole. "Do you believe in signs?"

Nicole was confused. "What, like astrology?"

"More like things unspoken, things the heart knows."

"I don't know."

"What is your name?"

"Nicole."

"A lovely name." She began to gather her things from Zooms' desk. "Perhaps we'll have a chance to speak again sometime, Nicole. I would like that." With a smile on her lips, Mrs. Litzger-Gold's eyes met Nicole's one last time. Then she walked out the classroom door.

CAUTION!!! WEBSITE UNDER CONSTRUCTION!!!

Day 4, 4:53 p.m.

Frightening Thought du Jour: I've never once seen my parents really kiss. What if the feeling of wanting someone so badly that you ache with wanting them always dies? What if all you get in its place is the married-and-live-happily-ever-after lie, which really means mortgages and dental bills and PTA meetings and nothing exciting for the rest of your entire life?

The Truth Hurts, So? H the Perfect can get J back because looks are power. Anyone who says that isn't true is lying. This is just the way it is.

The Truth Hurts, So? Part Two: The thoughts in my head are more interesting than the words on my lips. In school, with my family, every time I open my mouth, someone else speaks. Someone dull and ordinary. The only time I can transcend that is when I dance. Then I don't think. I just feel. I am the wind.

000001 MAGIC COUNTER

2
two

Despair. Nicole's pale face stared back at her in the mirror over her dresser: lank brown hair, boring brown eyes in a forgettable face, a body that was . . . a body. Not awful. But light-years from Heather the Perfect's.

Nicole pushed away the gloom. Winding her hair with a scrunchie, she padded over to her boom box, pressed ON, and danced. "One and two, three and four . . ." Watching herself move to the hip-hop groove, she tried a regulation Chrissy hair flip. Her ponytail whipped around and smacked her in the eye.

What was the use? What difference would it make if she changed the Fly Girls choreography a million times? True: Jack would see her dance at the talent show a week from Saturday. False: Seeing her dance would make him fall in love with her.

She turned off the music and threw herself onto her bed. It was a stupid dream. The dance was stupid. She was stupid.

Squee-eak. Scree-ech. Through the wall came the sounds of a violin being tortured.

Nicole pounded the wall. "Knock it off, Little Bit. I'm practicing in here."

Silence.

"Thank you." She set her jaw and went back to the mirror. Maybe dancing was a stupid dream, but it was the only dream she had. Hip-thrust one, hip-thrust two—

Renewed violin torture.

Nicole pounded the wall again. "Practice later, Little Bit, I mean it!"

Again. Focus. She moved to music inside her head, trying a facial expression that would tell Jack she was incredibly cool and incredibly hot at the same time. It looked okay in the mirror. She thrust her chest one way, her butt the other, and pursed her lips like a model.

Gales of laughter stopped her cold. "You look like a blowfish, Nicole." Little Bit stood in the doorway, violin under her arm.

"Have I mentioned what a brat you are?"

"Often." Her sister smiled sweetly. "Let's review. Mom said when I hit double digits you had to call me Elizabeth. And, happy birthday to me, I turned ten, two weeks ago. So call me Elizabeth."

"Get out of my room."

"Technically, I'm not *in* your room, I'm *outside* your room. Besides, if you don't want company, close your door."

Nicole swung the door shut.

"That wasn't very nice," Little Bit called.

Like she cared. It was just so irritating. Little Bit was everything wonderful that she was not—neat, organized, a straight-A student. Worse than that, Little Bit was a Heather-in-Training: gold hair, sky blue eyes fringed with sooty lashes. Worst of all, she knew it.

Suddenly, a terrible thought flitted into Nicole's mind. Like an unwanted, oblivious party guest, it wouldn't go away. She went to her computer, logged on to her website, then began to type.

NOTES FROM GIRL X

CAUTION!!! WEBSITE UNDER CONSTRUCTION!!!

Day 4, 6:43 p.m.

Frightening Thought du Jour, Part Two: My sister LB is ten, a junior H the Perfect. Soon, she'll be eleven. Twelve. Thirteen. The phone will ring. Guys will call. Cute guys. Guys like J who don't know I exist. And they will all be calling for her.

000001 MAGIC COUNTER

Pound, pound, pound on Nicole's door. "Dad wants to know if you're doing your homework."

Translation: Our father the college professor is planning to grill you for dinner.

"Did you hear me?" Little Bit called.

"Yes. Now go away." Nicole frowned. Why did their father insist on being one of those "involved" parents, which, from Nicole's point of view, simply meant that she was constantly being judged and found wanting? Her father would certainly ask her about English class. She needed to come up with two or three reasonably intelligent things to say about the Holocaust. Immediately.

No prob. She logged on to a big Internet search engine and typed the word *Holocaust*. There were 56,543 matches.

She scrolled down. Endless listings. Who knew there was so much? The Rhodes Jewish Museum on some island in Greece. The CDJC, the Centre de Documentation Juive Contemporaine, which was in French, her worst subject. What else? The Simon Wiesenthal Center's 36 Questions About the Holocaust . . .

"Nicole?" Little Bit called through the door.

"What?"

"Mom says dinner's in fifteen minutes."

"Fine."

"Can I come in?"

"No." Didn't Little Bit ever give up? Nicole clicked into the Wiesenthal Center site, scanning it quickly.

Knock-knock-knock.

"Little Bit, if you don't leave me alone—"

"It's *Elizabeth,* and I left my sweater in there before."

Nicole sighed. "Fine. Come in, get it, and then please give me a little peace and quiet."

Nicole scrolled down to the next site on the list: The Center for the Scientific Study of Genocide, whatever that was. At least it sounded intellectual. Intellectual always impressed her father. She surfed in and started to read.

The Center for the Scientific Study of Genocide
"Bringing the past into harmony with the truth."

If you would like to understand the revisionist viewpoint on history, you've come to the right website. The Center features revisionist studies about Auschwitz, Dachau, Nazi gas chambers, the Holocaust, and other aspects of history.

The "revisionist viewpoint on history"? It sounded technical. Suddenly Nicole got a terrific idea. What if she could find some kind of online summary of Anne Frank's diary? Like Cliff's Notes, only shorter? Then she wouldn't actually have to finish the book, and she'd have stuff to tell her father at dinner, too. She searched The Center's database under *Anne Frank*. A long list of scholarly-looking articles popped up. One caught her eye instantly.

Is Anne Frank's *Diary of a Young Girl* a fraud?

She clicked on the link. An article by someone named Arthur Favre popped up on her monitor.

Is Anne Frank's *Diary of a Young Girl* a fraud? I have been studying this question for three years, and have included it in my upper-level university seminar for the last eighteen months. I have concluded after much research that the diary of Anne Frank is a forgery.

"Who's Anne Frank?"

Nicole jumped. Little Bit was reading over her shoulder. "Why are you still here?"

"Because I didn't leave yet. Who's Anne Frank?"

"This Jewish girl who lived in Holland during World War Two," Nicole mumbled, as she scrolled further down the article. "When she was hiding from the Germans, she kept a diary. I have to read it for Bazooms' class."

Little Bit's jaw fell open. "You call your teacher *Bazooms*?"

"It's her name. Renee Zooms, middle initial B. Buh-Zooms." Nicole and her sister continued reading. Favre explained in the article how he'd scientifically determined that the diary was a forgery. He had dozens of impressively documented footnotes.

"So, if her diary is fake, why do you have to read it?" Little Bit asked.

"Got me." A sidebar link to something called Ask The Center's Experts came up. Nicole clicked, which took her to the center's online chat room. Without thinking much about it, she logged in as Girl X.

"Why do you call yourself Girl X?" Little Bit asked.

"You have two choices: Leave or be quiet."

The only other person in the chat room was a Dr. Bridgeman. A message from him popped up on her monitor.

DR. BRIDGEMAN: Hello, Girl X! And welcome to The Center. I'm Dr. Martin Bridgeman, the historian on duty this evening. How can I help you?

GIRL X: I'm not sure. I have to read Anne Frank's diary for high school. And I just read an article on this website that says it is a fake.

DR. BRIDGEMAN: Confusing, I know! Well, Girl X, the truth is that no one knows for sure. But during the 1950s, a Jewish man named Meyer Levin sued the writers of its movie version, claiming that they had stolen his work. And he won.

GIRL X: I never knew that.

DR. BRIDGEMAN: It's not one of the things they teach you in school.

GIRL X: Why not?

DR. BRIDGEMAN: A lot of educators feel guilty.

GIRL X: About what?

DR. BRIDGEMAN: The other side of the story. Did you know that our own government forced thousands of Japanese Americans into camps during WWII because we feared they'd be subversive? Germany did the same thing with their enemies. But we won the war, so we get to write history. It lessens our guilt to think that what Germany did was more awful than what we did.

GIRL X: But didn't the Germans kill millions of Jews during the Second World War?

DR. BRIDGEMAN: War is a terrible thing. Yes, a lot of innocent people on both sides died. Many were Jews, many were not. Are they also teaching you about the fire-bombing of Dresden by the Allies, for example?

"Who's Dresden?" Little Bit asked.

"Got me," Nicole muttered. She typed furiously.

GIRL X: I still don't get why anyone would publish a fake.

DR. BRIDGEMAN: Think about it, Girl X. It serves the interests of the people who don't want you to know the truth. There are still a lot of open questions about what happened during the war.

GIRL X: My teachers never said there were open questions.

DR. BRIDGEMAN: Don't be too hard on them. Sometimes it is difficult to look in the mirror. But the truth will come out in time. It always does. Just remember that there are two sides to every story. You believe that, don't you?

GIRL X: :)

DR. BRIDGEMAN: Smart girl. People go to death row for crimes they didn't commit; politicians that we elect lie to us. It's important for you to be an independent thinker. Get all the facts, then make up your own mind.

"Nicole! Elizabeth, dinner!" their mom called from downstairs.

GIRL X: I gotta go.

DR. BRIDGEMAN: Come back anytime, Girl X. There's always someone here who can help you with your research.

Nicole logged off.

"He was nice," Little Bit said.

"He was okay. I'll be down in a minute."

Little Bit bounded downstairs as Nicole went to wash her hands. She caught her reflection in the bathroom mirror, and for a split second, she saw the shining eyes of Mrs. Litzger-Gold looking back at her. She blinked. They were gone.

three

Nicole stopped in the archway of the dining room, watching her family as if they were strangers she'd come upon. The dimmed chandelier cast a golden glow on her father and Little Bit, who talked animatedly, leaning toward him like a flower to the sun.

" . . . and I would have gotten the highest grade, but Brian Lapsoll had all the vocabulary words written on his hand," Little Bit was saying.

Their mother carried a platter of chicken to the table. "Nicole, please sit. Elizabeth, did you tell your teacher?"

Little Bit shrugged as Nicole sat down. "Tattlers are the lowest."

"No, cheaters are the lowest," her father corrected, filling Little Bit's salad dish. "I'm seeing more and more plagiarized papers taken directly from research mills on the Internet. Cheaters deserve whatever punishment they get."

Reading about Anne Frank online instead of reading the diary would definitely meet her father's definition of cheating. Nicole forked a drumstick from the serving platter.

"Can I go to the mall with Britnee after school tomorrow, Mom?" Little Bit asked. "Her nanny can drive us if you can pick us up."

"How about riding your bicycle?" Dr. Burns suggested.

Little Bit looked askance. "Dad, no one rides their bike to the mall. So can you, Mom?"

"I'll have to check my schedule."

"If we had a nanny, you wouldn't have to check your schedule."

"Your mother and I prefer to raise our own children, thank you," her father said dryly.

"I just meant Mom wouldn't get so stressed."

"I'm not str—" Mrs. Burns began, just as her cell phone rang. "Mary Burns," she answered crisply. "Oh, hi, Dru . . . Yes . . . Yes . . . But that house is already in escrow! Hold a sec . . ." She covered the phone with her hand, mouthing apologies as she stepped away from the table.

Dr. Burns' mouth went tight. Nicole's father hated it when her mother interrupted "family time" with her work calls. Oblivious to the tension, Little Bit blithely continued eating. Nicole knew her sister couldn't remember a time when their mom wasn't working, when the family hadn't had plenty of money. But Nicole could. Seven years before, Mrs. Burns, who'd only attended junior college, had gotten her real estate license. It turned out that she was a real estate genius and now earned twice as much money as Dr. Burns did teaching college. The family had two new cars, a renovated kitchen, and had spent Christmas in Barbados. What was the point, Nicole thought, of her father—anyone—wasting all those years in school?

"Nicole?"

Her father was looking at her pointedly, which meant there had been a bunch of other words before that *Nicole.*

"Sorry?"

"I asked how things are going in French class."

"French?" He would have to ask about her worst subject. Nicole was pretty sure she'd bombed her most recent quiz. If she told him that, he'd ground her. She searched her mind frantically for something to distract him, but what?

Nicole's mother slid back into her seat. "I'm so sorry. But the buyer's lawyer called Dru to say—"

"Nicole was just about to tell us about French," her father interrupted.

"Oh, sorry, sweetie."

"Uh . . ." Nicole's mind was a complete blank. And then, it came to her. "Speaking of French, a French woman spoke to my English class today. She lived through the Holocaust." The family phone rang shrilly from multiple outlets.

"I'll get it!" Little Bit jumped up.

"Elizabeth, we don't interrupt family time for—" Dr. Burns began, but his daughter was already gone. He eyed his wife. "Now, who do you think she got that behavior from?"

"Mine are business calls, Liam." As if to illustrate the point, her cell phone rang again.

"Mary, really—"

She mouthed her apologies and strode to the kitchen, leaving Nicole and her father alone at the table. Dr. Burns began to slash at his chicken with little sawing motions. Obviously he had just entered the ticked-off zone, which meant that before he got ticked off at her, Nicole had to think of something to deflect him.

"Did I tell you that we're going on a field trip to the museum tomorrow, Dad?" she asked, her voice a bit too bright. "To the *Anne Frank in the World* exhibit."

He put down his fork and frowned. "It irritates me to no end that they saturate you kids with European material when you're completely ignorant about the literary legacy of your own country."

Bingo. She'd hit one of her dad's hot buttons.

"As I recall, you read two Holocaust novels when you were younger, didn't you? But you've never been assigned anything by, say, John Dos Passos? The U.S.A. trilogy?"

Nicole shook her head.

"He wrote during the Depression. Do you have any idea how terrible it was in America during the Depression? Honestly, Jews do not have a monopoly on suffering."

"I know, Dad." Agreeing with her father was always the safe choice.

Some killed themselves because the world had turned into a place in which they no longer wanted to live.

"Dad?" Nicole asked hesitantly. "Is it true that some Jews killed themselves?"

"Who killed themselves?" Little Bit scampered back into the dining room and plopped down in her seat. "Sorry, Daddy."

"How about some dessert?" Mrs. Burns asked, appearing in the doorway holding a tray of brownies. "I'm sorry about that call, it's just—"

"Nicole knows someone who killed herself," Little Bit reported.

"That's horrible," Mrs. Burns exclaimed, as she set the brownies on the table. "I read an article in *People* about how teen suicide is an epidemic. Who was it, honey?"

"No one you know," Nicole said softly. It was easier not to explain.

"Well, it's still a tragedy. Elizabeth, would you like a brownie before you load the dishwasher?"

"It's not my turn, it's her turn." Little Bit pointed at Nicole.

"Stop everything!" a voice commanded from the front hall. Mimi burst into the dining room. Pinned to her ratty-looking crocheted poncho was a yellow pin featuring a tearful baby harp seal, in protest against cruelty to animals.

"Oh, God, that poor chicken," Mimi said, eyeing the leftovers. Then she rallied. "Nico, we have to go to your room immediately. It's crucial."

Mrs. Burns smiled wryly. "Hello, Mimi, another understated entrance."

"Nicole can't leave, it's her night to load the dishwasher," Little Bit reported. "I made a chores chart to prove it."

30

"A chores chart?" Nicole echoed incredulously.

Mimi draped a gangly arm around Little Bit. "I've got a great idea. How about if you load the dishwasher and then you can give yourself a gold star on your little chores chart?"

"That's not fair. Mom—"

Mimi yanked Nicole out of the dining room. "Yes! A clean getaway," Nicole said, laughing, as they pounded upstairs to her room. She turned on her boom box. "Okay, about our choreography. I decided it's kind of lame when we—"

Mimi snapped off the music. "Forget Fly Girls. The opportunity of your life is about to come walking through that door."

At that moment, Suzanne walked in, dance bag slung over her shoulder. "Hey, what's up? Am I late? Your sister let me in."

Nicole eyed her dubiously. "Supposedly you're the opportunity of my life."

"Not *her*," Mimi insisted, grabbing Nicole's shoulders. "Would you please focus?"

"Fine. I'm focused. What?"

"Just now at the drugstore, I ran into the one and only J. Even as I speak, the one and only J is on his way over to the home of the one and only Girl X."

Nicole gulped. "Did you just say . . . ?"

"Who's Girl X?" Suzanne asked.

Mimi grinned. "She is."

Nicole was sure she couldn't have heard what she thought she had heard. Amazing how loud wishful thinking could be. "Meem . . . you aren't telling me that Jack Polin—"

"I am telling you." Mimi's eyes shone, and she hugged Nicole hard. "Nico, your dream is about to come true."

f o u r

I have nothing to wear," Nicole moaned.

"Right, you only own half the clothes in the mall." Mimi pawed through Nicole's closet. She considered a skimpy camisole. "Nah. Screams of trying too hard."

"Hurry up, Meem," Nicole muttered. "He's gonna be here any minute." She bit nervously at a hangnail.

"Are you and Jack a thing?" Suzanne asked. "I thought he and Heather—"

"Ancient history," Mimi reported. "Nicole and Jack are an about-to-be thing. He has a massive crush on her."

Nicole snorted. "Yeah, right."

"This. This is it." Mimi held up a little floral dress. "It's perfect. Demure, yet sexy—"

"I never wear that. I look like a cow in that."

"You do not, do not argue, go put it on," Mimi insisted.

Nicole grabbed the dress and hurried to the bathroom. Off came the sweats, on went the dress. She looked in the full-length mirror to see if she looked fat. She did. "Okay, you look like barf," she told her reflection.

33

Two sharp raps sounded on the bathroom door. "Nico, he's here," Mimi hissed. "And he's with Eddie. Move it!"

Oh, God. No time to change. Stuck in her fat dress, Nicole tore the scrunchie from her hair and got to her room just as Mimi and Suzanne were shoving the last of her mess into her closet.

"I am so fat," Nicole moaned. "Someone please starve me."

"You're not fat," Mimi said. "Sit down. And act natural."

Nicole heard Jack and Eddie talking sports as they came down the hallway. She struck a nonchalant pose on a chair as Little Bit ushered them into the room.

"It's usually messier than this," Little Bit informed them. "Things actually grow under my sister's bed."

Jack's easy smile lit up his face. "Hey. Nice house."

"Thanks." Nicole tried to match his offhand tone. "So, what's up with you guys?"

"Same old same old, you know," Eddie replied.

"We're rehearsing. For the talent show thing," Mimi said.

"If we're interrupting—" Jack began.

"No, no, you're not!" Nicole insisted. She took a deep breath and forced herself back into casual mode. "I mean, we were just taking a break, anyway."

Little Bit shined her thousand-watt smile at Jack. "I neglected to introduce myself. I'm Nicole's sister, Elizabeth."

Jack looked amused. "Hello, Elizabeth. How old are you?"

"Older than I look." Little Bit executed a perfect regula-

34

tion Chrissy hair toss. Excruciating. Her little sister was flirting with Jack.

Nicole jumped up. "You were just leaving, Little Bit." She pointed her sister toward the door, then turned back to Jack. "Sorry. I know she's a pain in the—"

"Oh my gosh, Nicole!" Little Bit shrieked.

Nicole spun around. "What?"

"The back of your—"

"What?" Instinctively, Nicole reached behind her. Instead of hitting dress, she felt nothing but bulging panties. While she was changing clothes, she had somehow stuffed the hem of her dress inside her panties. Oh, God. She yanked her dress out and smoothed it down. Too late. Eddie was falling all over himself laughing, which meant he and Jack had seen everything. She wasn't even wearing cute bikinis—she had on the baggy old-lady panties her mom had bought her.

"Those are the butt-ugliest undies I ever saw!" Eddie gasped, between peals of laughter. Burning with humiliation, Nicole dropped down on her bed and stared at the polished wood floor as if there was something there worth seeing.

"Oh, Eddie, grow up," Mimi chided him. "What are you, six?"

Nicole risked a peek at the guys. Tears of mirth were rolling down Eddie's cheeks.

"Cut it out," Jack told him, but it was obvious he was trying not to laugh, too.

"You could go snow-blind from lookin' at those two big ol' white moons, man," Eddie howled.

"My sister does *not* have a big moon butt!" Little Bit insisted, which made Eddie convulse anew.

Jack flicked his hand against Eddie's back. "Like you've never done anything embarrassing. How about when you came out on the soccer field trailing, like, a yard of toilet paper?"

"That's cold, Polin."

Little Bit folded her arms. "You deserved it, Eddie. You were being extremely immature."

Great. Her little sister was defending her. Nicole wanted to crawl into her closet with the rest of her mess.

Mimi spotted Nicole's copy of Anne Frank's diary on her desk, and picked it up. "Read this yet?"

"Got it covered." Eddie smirked. "Saw it on cable."

Mimi groaned. "You are such a Neanderthal. It happens to be amazing."

"It is, I read it last year," Suzanne agreed.

Little Bit grabbed the book from Mimi. "Does it have any dirty parts?" She started flipping through the pages.

"Yo, aren't you a little young for that?" Eddie asked.

"I happen to be extremely mature for my age."

"I'm only, like, thirty pages into it so far," Jack said.

"Me, too," Nicole agreed. "Who has time?"

"Oh my gosh, listen to this!" Little Bit exclaimed. " 'We are shut up here, shut away from the world, in fear and anxiety, especially just lately. Why, then, should we who love each

36

other remain apart? Why should we wait until we've reached a suitable age? Why should we bother?' "

"No way was that in the movie," Eddie said.

Little Bit shrugged. "What difference does it make? "It's a big fake. Anne Frank didn't even write it."

"Ignore her," Nicole pleaded. "It's just some stupid thing we saw on the Internet. She's trying to show off."

"I am not." Little Bit folded her arms defiantly. "That man was a historian, Nicole. He knows way more than you do."

Jack tugged playfully at Little Bit's ponytail. "Go, girl. Don't let 'em dis you. Think for yourself."

Little Bit shot Nicole a smug look. "Well, *some* people don't care about thinking for themselves."

"Yo, whatever," Eddie said. "Who cares?"

"So listen," Jack began. "About the talent show thing. Maybe at the party afterwards, the five of us could hook up. You up for it?" He looked at Nicole.

Her stomach bungee-jumped with happiness. She went for casual. "Sounds fun."

Jack's face lit up. "Yeah? Great!"

Nicole executed a regulation Chrissy hair toss, batted her eyelashes, and smiled seductively. For once, she pulled it off. She felt poised on the cliff of possibility, ready to spread her wings for the first time. And fly.

CAUTION!!! WEBSITE UNDER CONSTRUCTION!!!

Day 4, 11:25 p.m.

. . . and that is exactly what happened. God, life is so weird. One minute, I'm dying of embarrassment 'cuz J saw my putrid panties. The next minute I'm dying of happiness 'cuz he asked me to hang out after the talent show.

Girl in the Middle: After everyone left, I looked at myself in the mirror. I was so much cuter than I had been just a few hours before. What is it: amazing, scary, or wonderful, how quickly your life can change?

Bliss: I will remember what happened today for the rest of my life. Today is the day I was transformed by love.

Heavy Ick Factor: Transformed by love???

Frightening Thought du Jour, Part Three: If love transforms, then who was I when neediness oozed off me like stale sweat? When J didn't know I existed, it made me feel like I didn't exist. Color me pathetic, boys and girls.

Tomorrow: I will see J.
Tonight: He will make love to me in my dreams.

5
five

Nicole scanned the faces of the crowd in front of her school. "Do you see Jack?"

Mimi cocked her chin. "Right over there."

Nicole spotted him. He was with a bunch of his jock friends near the flagpole. "He hasn't even acknowledged my existence. Maybe last night was a figment of my vivid imagination."

Mimi unwrapped a stick of bubble gum and curled it into her mouth. "He's into you, Nico."

"How do you know?"

"Okay, I know I'm the one who gave love a jump-start here, but I gotta tell you, Nico, on the lame-o-meter scale of one to ten, your thing about Jack is pushing elev—"

"He's looking at me," Nicole hissed, as Jack's eyes caught hers. He nodded and smiled, then went back to his friends. She grabbed Mimi's arm. "Did you see that?"

"No. I was struck blind by the miracle of it all." Mimi blew a bubble.

"Morning."

Nicole turned around. David Berg stood there, a crooked smile on his face. In sixth grade, they'd worked together at the library on a science project. They'd talked for hours about everything; he'd had a crush on her since then that rivaled hers on Jack. Nicole had no idea why. She liked him, but he wasn't Jack.

"Hey," Nicole said.

"So . . . this exhibit should be great. I went to the Secret Annex in Amsterdam last summer. It was amazing."

Nicole looked beyond his shoulder at Jack. "What's that?"

"Where Anne Frank and her family hid from the Nazis?" David asked with exasperation. "Ring any bells?"

"Oh. Sure." Nicole forced herself to focus on David.

"Why do you do that?" His dark eyes probed hers.

"Do what?"

"Blow off reading like you're an airhead, when you're not."

Nicole shrugged. How could she possibly care about something as trivial as a book right now?

"Unreal," David muttered. "I don't believe it."

"What?"

He pointed at Doom, who was hanging out near the curb with three of his identically dressed friends. The Doom Squad, everyone called them. "I can't believe he showed for this."

"Me, neither," Mimi agreed.

David's eyes narrowed. "His walls are probably covered with Hitler memorabilia."

"Come on, lighten up," Nicole said. But when she looked over at Doom, she felt uneasy, too.

David's gaze swung back to Nicole and he cleared his throat nervously. "So, Nicole, maybe we could sit together on the—"

"Nicole?" She felt the lightest touch on her shoulder. Him. She gazed up into Jack's electric blue eyes. "Listen, can we sit together on the bus? I really want to talk to you."

"Sure."

"Great."

Dizzy with happiness, she watched Jack stride back to his friends. Then Zooms' voice got her attention as David drifted away. "Burns, Berg, Gullet, Polin, McPhee," the teacher read, checking names off her list. "The rest of you will be on the next bus. Lee, Simmons, Baker, et cetera."

"Now I won't get to watch you and Jack," Mimi moped.

"What if he forgets he asked me to sit with him?"

"Since you can't seem to retain this, I say we tattoo it on your butt: *Jack likes Nicole.* It's so sixth grade."

"Please board your buses in an orderly fashion," John Urkin, the new high school principal, called through a bull-horn.

From the crowd, Eddie taunted, "Urk-urk-urk-Urkin!"

"He's such a butthole," Mimi told Nicole.

"Who, Urkin?"

"Eddie. Someone told me Urkin was a medic in Vietnam. He risked his life and has a bunch of medals or something."

Nicole regarded her balding, middle-aged, soft-spoken

41

principal, who stood near the flagpole with his bullhorn. "I don't think so. I mean, look at the guy."

"I'm looking. Think he's ever had sex?"

"More often than we have," Nicole replied. Mimi laughed.

"Miss Burns, kindly go board your bus," Zooms ordered. "Miss Baker, kindly move it."

By the time Nicole reached her bus, it was already full. The only empty seat was near the back. Next to Jack. He had saved it for her. She felt helium-balloon buoyant as she walked down the aisle, passing couples on both sides of her. Now, she was part of a couple, too.

"'S great getting sprung from school, huh?" Jack asked, as she slid into the seat next to him.

"Definitely."

His fingers drummed on the leg of his jeans as the bus pulled out. "So, how's your dance thing coming along?"

"Judge for yourself when you see it."

"Last year you and Mimi had a different girl dancing in the group, didn't you?"

"Yeah." Jack had noticed that her trio had danced in last year's talent show. Shocking. That meant he'd had his eye on her for a long time. How could she have been so oblivious? "Sara Cambridge," Nicole continued. "She moved to Florida. Suzanne's better anyway. We might make an audition tape for MTV."

"Oh, yeah? Cool." Jack hesitated. "Nicole, there's something I've been wanting to tell you—"

"Go ahead," Nicole encouraged, as the bus turned onto the interstate.

"I feel like I can really talk to you."

"You can," she assured him.

"Yeah." He ran his fingers through his hair and leaned his head back on the seat. "I can't believe how hard this is."

How sweet was he? That a guy like him could have such a hard time talking about his feelings for a girl like her made her love him even more. She put her hand lightly on his arm. "Jack? You can tell me anything. Really."

Then it happened. He put an arm around her shoulders and leaned closer. "I wanted to say something to you at your house last night," he admitted, his voice low, "but—I should just come out and say it. Right?"

She nodded. Their eyes met, in unspoken union.

"Nicole," he whispered into her ear.

"Yes?"

"It's about . . ."

"Yes?"

"It's about Suzanne. I'm crazy about her."

The world turned upside down. "You . . . what?"

"I think about her all the time, it's really crazy. So I wanted to ask you, since you're friends with her and everything. Could you find out if she likes me?"

"You want me to—"

"I know it's lame," he rushed on. "She's so gorgeous. And really nice, don't you think? But when I'm around her, I'm so freaked I can't even look at her. So—I know it's a lot

43

to ask—could you be a friend and find out if she likes me at all?"

"Yeah. Sure." Nicole bit the inside of her lip; a trickle of blood oozed into her mouth.

"That's great, Nicole. Thanks. I mean it."

He enveloped her in the hug she had dreamt about for so long. It was everything she wanted. And, at the same time, exactly what she knew she would never, ever have.

six

It's about Suzanne.

Dozens of buses from various schools were parked outside the state museum, including some from East High, West's big rivals, as more than a thousand kids waited to be admitted into the museum. One of them was Nicole; there, but not there.

I'm crazy about her.

"West High students, attention, please." Mr. Urkin was using his bullhorn again. "We need everyone's cooperation. It will take approximately two hours to go through the Anne Frank exhibit. Following that, we'll visit the permanent collection of the state museum." Coach Carr whispered something to Mr. Urkin, who reluctantly raised the bullhorn to his lips again. "And yes, we'll be back at school in time for our football team to prepare for the game tomorrow against East High's Lions."

Coach Carr pumped his fist in the air. "Eat 'em, Bears!" he shouted. West's kids cheered. Across the plaza, the East students booed lustily. Nicole was only dimly aware, as if she were half-watching a television show she wasn't much interested in. Jack's words played over and over in her mind, a wound etched on her heart.

Mr. Urkin made another announcement—that one of the buses had a flat tire and would be late. They'd begin the tour anyway. Mimi's bus, Nicole thought dully. That's why she isn't here.

Zooms beckoned to her students. "Shake a leg, people. Move in close so you can all hear me."

Someone touched her arm. David. "Nicole? You okay?"

"Fine." Her masochistic eyes sought out Jack. He was in the center of a crowd, laughing at something Eddie had just said. It hurt to look at him. It hurt not to. He had no idea that he'd just smashed her heart into a million pieces. The funny thing was, Nicole knew he'd feel terrible if he knew. But it still wouldn't make him love her. Nothing would.

Zooms edged closer to her students. "Listen up, because I will not be repeating myself. We're going inside now. Your late classmates will join us there. I've prepared something special for you. You will each receive an envelope with your name on it. Inside, you'll find your new identity for the duration of this tour. All of you are about to become contemporaries of Anne Frank."

The students stood impassively as Zooms held up a fistful of envelopes. "Some of you will live, and some of you will die. Some of you will hide, some of you will hide others. Some of you will be shot. Many of you will be deported. You may watch your family members march to their deaths. Some of you will be gassed." A hush came over the group.

"At the end of our experience today," Zooms continued, "you'll receive another envelope. Only then will you discover what happened to you; if you lived or if you died." She began barking out last names in a military fashion. One by one the students got their envelopes.

"Burns." Zooms handed Nicole an envelope with her name on it. She opened it.

> You are a Jewish girl named Nicole Bernhardt. You were born in 1927 in Paris, France, and you still live there. You have a sister who is five years younger. Your parents are Renée and Jean. Your father is a famous doctor. You are a smart girl but you do not like school; you are outgoing, popular, and a wonderful dancer, and you can play the piano. The year is now 1942. You are fifteen years old.

All around Nicole, her classmates read their biographies.

"Listen, are you sure you're okay, Nicole?" David asked her again. "You're really pale."

"I'm fine. Please stop asking me that." She got into one of the lines snaking toward the entrance, David right behind her. She was hyperaware of Jack, in the next line.

So, could you be a friend and find out if she likes me at all?

Yeah, sure.

David looked to see who had Nicole's attention and spotted Jack. "Figures," he mumbled.

Security at the museum was tight. The students had to pass a gauntlet of six burly men clad in dark suits, with earpieces and small microphones on their lapels. Nicole moved forward, staring at the angel tattoo on the back of Julie Needers' neck. Her boyfriend, Peter something-or-other, draped an arm over the tattoo. "Hey, Jul, check those dudes out. Jewish Gestapo," he said.

"Not funny," Julie snapped.

Peter gave a mock Nazi salute to the security detail, who didn't react. Julie poked him. "Cut it out, I mean it. You want people to think you're in the Doom Squad?"

"Well, what is up with this?" Peter groused. "Do they think we're gonna blow up the exhibit?"

"All it takes is one idiot," David insisted, loud enough for everyone to hear. "You wanna risk that?"

"Whatever. If we don't kick East's butt tomorrow, I'm gonna blow up the football field," Peter joked. David didn't smile. "Yo, David, it's a joke. Chill out."

Nicole put her backpack on the conveyor through the X-ray machine. From the next line: *BEEP! BEEP! BEEP!* She looked to see who had set off the metal detector. Doom. An imposing security guard stepped over to him. "Young man, please step this way and put your feet on the marks on the floor."

The crowd buzzed as Doom hit the proper marks, arms

out to the sides. He stared blankly as the guard passed a metal-sensitive wand over him. "Hey, make sure you get the plate in his head," Eddie cracked.

"Go on, young man, you're fine," the security guard told Doom. "It was the grommets on your boots."

The crowd dispersed; Nicole spotted Zooms in front of a large photograph with white lettering. Anne Frank. She trudged over and idly read the caption.

SINCE ITS FIRST PUBLICATION IN 1947, MILLIONS OF PEOPLE AROUND THE WORLD HAVE READ THE DIARY OF ANNE FRANK, GIVING A SUCCESSION OF NEW GENERATIONS A PENETRATING LOOK AT THE PERSECUTION OF THE JEWS DURING WORLD WAR II. WHAT WAS IT LIKE TO BE A JEWISH CHILD HIDING IN THE NETHERLANDS DURING THE NAZI OCCUPATION? WHAT WAS IT LIKE TO GO THROUGH EVERY MINUTE OF THE DAY AFRAID OF BEING DISCOVERED, AND WONDERING WHAT WOULD HAPPEN AFTERWARD? ANNE FRANK, HER FAMILY AND A FEW OF THEIR FRIENDS SPENT MORE THAN TWO YEARS HIDDEN IN THE SECRET ANNEX. A FEW OF HER FATHER'S EMPLOYEES HELPED THEM, THEREBY RISKING THEIR OWN LIVES.

"Amazing, isn't it?" David asked, joining her.

Not again, Nicole thought. Can't he just leave me alone?

"I guess Mimi's on the bus with the flat," he added.

Mimi. How was she ever going to tell Mimi about Jack? And Suzanne? Suzanne and Jack would become a couple and they'd feel so sorry for her because she had been pathetic enough to believe that Jack—

Suddenly, Nicole knew that she could not take one more minute of standing there, pretending that her entire life hadn't just been ruined. "Excuse me," she blurted out, spotting the sign for the ladies' room. "I have to—"

She took off. "Miss Bernhardt!" It vaguely registered that Zooms was calling her by her new identity. But Nicole didn't stop. All she could think of was escape. She burst into the ladies' room and collided with a girl on her way out.

"Sorry."

"Hey, Nicole, it's me."

It was Claire Levin, who lived three doors down from the Burnses. They'd been friends until third grade; then Claire's parents had enrolled her in a private Jewish academy. "Did you come with your school?" Claire asked.

Nicole nodded.

"So, how are you?" Claire asked eagerly. She had the same chubby cheeks she'd had as a little girl, the same mop of red curls. "It's so funny, running into you like this. I was just thinking—"

"Sorry, I'm sick," Nicole interrupted, rushing into a stall and locking it behind her.

"Nicole?" Claire called. "Is there someone you want me to get for you?"

"No. Thanks."

"I'll wait. To make sure you're okay."

"No. I mean, I'm all right. You can go."

"Are you sure?"

"Yeah."

"Okay, I'll call you."

Moments later, Nicole heard the click of the ladies' room door as Claire left. Then, in that tiny oasis of privacy that smelled of pine cleanser, with KARA IS A FAT PIG scrawled on the wall, she let the tears come.

〜

Nicole heard the bathroom door open. "Nico?"

Mimi. She'd recognize the voice anywhere.

"I'm in here."

"David said you're sick. You okay?"

Nicole closed her eyes. "I feel better now," she lied.

"Get your butt out here, then. You have to tell me what happened with Jack. And Zooms is on the warpath." Nicole flushed the toilet for show, then came out to wash her hands.

"What's wrong?" Mimi asked.

"Nothing."

"Nico, this is me you're talking to. What is it? Killer cramps? Pregnant by Immaculate Conception? Work with me, here."

"I'm fine. Let's just go." Nicole half ran out the door and across the museum rotunda back to their group, Mimi hurrying to keep up with her.

"What is *up* with you, Nico?"

"It's not important."

"Mademoiselle Bernhardt, nice of you to rejoin us," Zooms said dryly. "So glad it fit into your schedule."

A middle-aged woman wearing a white blouse and black skirt stood before the group. "If I could have your attention. Welcome to the *Anne Frank in the World* exhibit. I'm Marta Wilk and I'll be guiding your visit. This way, please."

As they followed their guide, Mimi grabbed Nicole's arm. "Nicole, what's going on?"

"I told you—"

"No, you blew me off. Did something happen with Jack?"

Nicole hesitated. Mimi was her best friend. She could tell her the truth. "Yeah. Something happened."

"On the bus, you mean?"

Nicole nodded. "He saved me a seat. I sat with him, and—"

"Hey, you guys," Suzanne called, catching up to them. "Did Mimi tell you about our little adventure while the bus was being fixed? Ms. Farmer had an asthma attack, and—"

"We were talking about something else," Mimi said sharply. Nicole flicked her eyes at Suzanne, signaling Mimi that what she'd been about to say was private. Mimi nodded. Nicole was happy for the reprieve. Telling Mimi would somehow make it even truer.

Their group stopped before a triangular unit covered with text and photos. "We begin in 1929," Ms. Wilk said. "This photograph of Anne as a baby, in her mother's arms, was taken soon after she was born. You will note that—"

A cheerleader ran over and interrupted the guide. "Ms. Zooms, Ms. Farmer is having another attack and her inhaler quit. She said I should get you."

"Stay with Ms. Wilk," Zooms ordered her students. "I'll catch up." But as soon as Zooms was out of sight, kids began slipping away from the group. Doom and his Doom Squad headed farther into the exhibit hall. Eddie announced he had to hit the john and took off laughing with Peter.

Ms. Wilk led what was left of the class toward the next photograph. "We come now to a photograph from Germany, 1932. This shows how terrible things can often start out very small. It is a poster for an early political campaign of Adolf Hitler. It reads, in German, 'Hitler—our last hope.' "

Mimi nudged Nicole. "Nico, quick. Suzanne's back there, talking to David. So tell me what happened with—"

CRACK!

CRACK! CRACK! CRACK! CRACK!

The sound of gunfire echoed through the exhibition hall. Panic struck. Screaming people ran in every direction and dove for cover. "Doom's shooting!" someone yelled. "Doom's got a gun!"

Nicole found herself running toward an exit sign as a piercing alarm sounded. A wave of students pushed her from behind, slamming her against a wall.

Mimi yanked her arm. "Come on!" She pulled Nicole away from the wall, but they were nearly trampled by a line of security guards, guns drawn, charging toward the sound of the shots.

More screams, more crying. The air was thick with the smell of gunpowder. Nicole and Mimi were trapped in a mass of students jamming the emergency exit. "Help me!" a girl screamed, as she fell in the crush. A boy stepped on her arm and ran on.

"Mimi!"

"Hold on, Nico!"

Nicole grabbed her friend's hand. "Don't let go!" They were being pushed from all sides.

"Nico, I can't—"

Nicole felt Mimi's hand slipping from hers. "Don't fall!" she ordered, as if her voice could keep her friend up. Mimi let go. "Mimi! Where are you? Mimi!"

CRACK! CRACK! CRACK!

A sudden pain pierced Nicole, red-hot. And then, there was nothing at all.

s e v e n

The blaring high-pitched whine of sirens. A terrible pounding inside her head. Raw, rhythmic waves of pain. Nicole clamped her hands over her eyes and moaned. It was as if her mind were swimming through muck, coming up from another place. Who and where she was, and what had happened, returned to her slowly, like faces materializing on a developing photograph.

The state museum. Doom. Gunfire. Panic. Death.

Like TV news footage, images played inside her mind— SWAT teams, police setting a perimeter so the shooter couldn't escape, innocents led away by teachers, ambulances lined up like soldiers at inspection. Inside the museum— Oh, God. Bodies everywhere, bleeding on the floor.

But this wasn't television, live from Colorado or Oregon or Georgia. It was happening in her state, to her classmates. To her.

Nicole felt the pull of unconsciousness lulling her back to safety. Fight, she told herself. Focus. What else must be happening? Had the television trucks arrived? Helicopters?

Were they talking about Doom, showing his picture from the ninth-grade yearbook on the air? What if he still had a gun? My parents must be worried. Maybe they're on their way with Mimi's parents. Mimi. Caught in the crush. I have to make sure Mimi is okay.

That last thought got Nicole to open her eyes; fast, like a bandage ripped off in one quick move. She struggled to rise; strong hands on her shoulders held her in place. "Mimi," she mumbled. "Got to find Mimi." She looked up. The eyes of Mr. Urkin looked back.

"Rest now," he told her. Ms. Zooms' face loomed cartoon-ishly near his.

"Doom has a gun. We have to get out of here!" Her own voice hurt her head as much as the sirens. She struggled to stand, but Urkin gently pressed her to the couch. Couch? That had to mean she wasn't on the floor of the museum anymore. Someone—Zooms, Urkin, both of them?—must have rescued her.

She turned to see where she was and the movement felt like a punch to the skull. Weird. She seemed to be in someone's living room. The upholstered furniture was old-fashioned, a grandfather clock stood in one corner, a grand piano faced one wall, and above it hung Impressionist paintings like those her French teacher always raved about.

So, where was she? In a museum room that had been made to look like Anne Frank's home? Possibly. But if she and Urkin and Zooms were safe, why weren't more people with them?

"Where's Doom? Did the cops get him?" She touched her cheek, which was throbbing. It was bandaged, wet to the touch. She looked at her finger. "I'm bleeding."

"Just a scratch," Urkin said.

"Did Doom shoot me? He did, didn't he? That's why you look so worried."

"What is she talking about?" Zooms asked, as Urkin took a little light from a black bag and shined it in her eyes.

"A concussion," he concluded. "It can be very disorienting. I do not know if she even knows where she is."

"Of course I know where I am," Nicole insisted. "I'm in the state museum. Now, what happened to Mimi? And Doom?"

"Doom?" Zooms echoed. In a flash, Nicole realized what was going on. Bazooms didn't know who Doom was.

"Richard Hayden," she explained. "We all call him Doom." Zooms still looked at her blankly. How could she be so dense? Nicole lay there, frustrated, her head throbbing, as the sirens diminished and finally stopped. The silence was a gift.

"No more sirens, they must have got him," Nicole concluded. "Can I go now?"

"John, this is breaking my heart," Zooms said. John? Since when did Zooms call Urkin by his first name in front of a student?

Urkin took a pocket watch from his vest and timed her pulse. "Seventy beats per minute. Your heart is beating wonderfully."

"Great to hear. It's really nice of you to be so concerned about me," Nicole told him. "But can we just go? Everyone must think we're dead."

Zooms' hand flew to her mouth as if Nicole had just let fly a string of colorful profanities in class. That was it. Nicole couldn't take any more. *"Let's go!"* She pushed Urkin's hands away and stood up. Sharp pain exploded in her head. She moaned and slumped back down.

Urkin began to stroke her hair. Very strange. It felt good, though. "Just rest now," he told her.

"But—"

"Rest."

"At least tell me what happened, please."

"You fell and hit your head," Zooms explained.

"I know that. I mean, what happened to everyone else?"

"I think her brain is damaged." Zooms gave Urkin a look of pure anguish. "She talks about this *doom* like it is a person."

Nicole felt like screaming. "Not an *it,* a *he.* I *told* you, *Richard Hayden.*"

Zooms touched Nicole's hand. "Do you know your name?"

"I'm wounded, not stupid. My name is Nicole."

"Good." Urkin nodded, and a strange thought crossed Nicole's mind. A teen on a shooting rampage at the museum would be a big story. And she'd been shot. Did that mean she'd be interviewed on CNN?

"And your last name is—" Zooms coaxed.

Nicole sighed irritably. "Burns."

"Bernhardt," Zooms corrected. "I am your mother, and this is your father."

Nicole had to laugh, even though it hurt. They were definitely not her parents. And Nicole Bernhardt was the name on the biography sheet that Zooms had handed her when they were still outside the museum.

"Why are you laughing, little one?" Urkin asked.

Little one? "I am laughing," Nicole began deliberately, "because you are my principal, Mr. Urkin. And she is my English teacher, Ms. Zooms. And Zooms named me Bernhardt. For the museum thing."

Zooms turned to Urkin. "Do something," she demanded.

"Do you have any idea where you are?" her principal asked. "Do you know that you're in Paris?"

"Paris? Paris, *France*?"

"Very good." Urkin sounded relieved. "See, Renée, she knows where she is."

"Right. If this is Paris, France, what language am I speaking?" Nicole challenged.

"French, of course."

"Ha! I'm practically flunking French."

The two adults stared at her blankly.

"Okay, that's it, I'm gone." Nicole tried to stand again, but the pain was overwhelming. "My head's killing me," she moaned.

"Liz-Bette?" Urkin called. "Bring some ice for your sister!"

"Wait a second," Nicole protested. "My sister isn't here."

"Of course I'm here," a familiar voice responded. "I have ice. I chipped it from the icebox."

Her sister was standing before her, carrying a towel-wrapped bundle. "Little Bit?" Nicole asked, stunned. "What are you doing here?"

"Liz-Bette," her sister corrected, as Zooms took the bundle from her. "Is she all right?"

"A concussion, your father thinks," Zooms said. She pressed the ice to Nicole's forehead. Nicole winced.

"You were dancing down the stairs from the roof," Urkin told Nicole. "The railing broke; you hit your head."

Nicole barely heard the explanation. Instead, she stared at Little Bit, who looked truly strange. First of all, her hair was neatly braided. Little Bit would rather chew glass than wear braids. Then there was her outfit. Little Bit had a closet full of trendy clothes. But she now wore a calf-length plaid skirt and a white shirt buttoned to her neck, under a navy cardigan. On her feet were very worn shoes. With white socks.

"It serves you right, Nicole," Little Bit admonished. "Dancing on the stairs after Maman told you not to a hundred times was extremely immature."

"Different clothes, same brat. And what is that thing?" She pointed at a yellow star sewn over the heart of Little Bit's sweater. It was fist-sized, but it didn't have five points like the one that went on top of a Christmas tree. It had six points. On the star were the letters Juif.

"Ha-ha, very funny." Little Bit smirked.

"It's the Nazis' star for the Jews," Zooms explained. "You have one, too."

"There is no way I—" Nicole looked down when she felt something sewn to the left side of her sweater. A star just like Little Bit's. On a gray sweater she didn't own.

Pain pulsed again inside Nicole's head. "Just a minute. Do you mean to tell me that I'm Jewish?"

"Of course," Mr. Urkin replied. "We are all Jewish."

Nicole held both hands to her head. The pulsing grew louder and louder; she didn't feel as if her skull could contain it. "You have to tell me." Her own voice sounded distant to her ears, like she was at the bottom of a well. "What year is it?"

The moan of the sirens began again. "Nineteen forty-two, my darling child," Urkin said. "Nineteen forty-two."

e**i**g**h**t

June 15, 1942

Possibilities for What Is Happening to Me

    1. Doom shot me and I am dead and in Hell.

    2. Doom shot me and I'm alive but in a coma and my mind is playing tricks on me while I'm unconscious.

    3. Doom did not shoot me, but I got crushed trying to get out the exit, am unconscious, see #2 above.

    4. It is still the night before the school trip and this is all a dream. Correction. A nightmare. The kind where you tell yourself to wake up only you can't wake up so you think it's real, but it isn't.

Nicole sat at the grand piano and plunked out a melody with one finger. She had no idea what it was. "What I'm experiencing here is a *Close Encounters of the Third Kind* moment," she muttered to herself. "A really long one."

Thinking about *Close Encounters* gave her an idea, though. The night before, she'd lain on a feather mattress in a strange bedroom with cabbage-rose-patterned wallpaper. Bazooms had insisted it was her room. But it wasn't. Not only did it look nothing at all like her bedroom, but this room was neat and her room was a disaster area. Sleep was impossible because of the sirens, which her sister claimed were warnings about British bombers. So she'd made a mental list of what was happening to her. Now, even as she tinkled the piano keys, she added a fifth possibility.

5. I have been abducted by aliens.

She'd been certain that if she could only fall asleep, she'd wake up in her own bedroom in the twenty-first century. But when she'd actually awakened to warm sunlight streaming through her window, she was still in the other place: Paris, during the Nazi Occupation, living the life that Ms. Zooms had assigned her for the *Anne Frank in the World* exhibit.

Logically, she knew that couldn't be true, which gave her another idea.

6. At the exhibit I was drugged and am now being used as a guinea pig in some weird social-science experiment. Hidden cameras are videotaping me all the time.

That could be it. She jumped up and began to look behind the living room paintings, in search of hidden cameras.

"Nicole? What are you doing?" Ms. Zooms looked up from her newspaper.

"Finding the hidden cameras."

Ms. Zooms patted the couch next to her. "Come here, Nicole."

"Thanks, but no thanks." Nicole moved a still life oil painting. There was nothing there.

"Nicole, I will tell you once again. I am your mother, Renée Bernhardt."

"I heard you the last ten times. Want proof? Mr. Urkin is my dear old dad, only his real name is Dr. Jean Bernhardt, a doctor at the Rothschild Hospital on something called rue Picpus," she recited. "What is a Picpus, anyway?"

"You're babbling again, Nicole."

"Yeah. Like what you're saying makes perfect sense. I'm telling you, I'm American. I live in the twenty-first century."

"I am trying not to worry. It is difficult," Ms. Zooms told her. "Your father says it may take some time for your memory to return. But when my daughter believes she is an American from the future, this is not a concussion. This is insanity."

"Look, Ms. Zooms, you've got to stop calling me your daughter." Nicole sat at the piano again and plunked out the same melody. "I mean, think about it. You don't even like me."

Ms. Zooms—Ms. Bernhardt—whatever her name was—gasped, even though Nicole could tell she was trying to do what Mr. Urkin—Dr. Bernhardt—whatever his name was—had told her to do in front of Nicole: Act as normal as possible.

"Why not really play the Smetana?" Zooms asked.

"Because I have no idea what *Smetana* is. Also, not knowing how to play the piano kind of gets in the way of actually playing it."

"Of course you know how to play the piano."

"No, I don't. I used to play flute in the geek-fest school orchestra, but I sucked so bad my parents let me quit."

"I shall prove to you that you know how to play the piano. Do not go anywhere." Ms. Zooms hurried from the room.

Nicole stared at the piano keys. She vaguely recalled that the ninth-grade orchestra teacher had taught her how to play a major scale. You had to start on the note C, but she had no idea which key was—

Her index finger pressed a key. C. She knew it, though she didn't know how she knew it. Then, even though she felt ridiculous, she cupped both hands over the keyboard.

Too bad this isn't one of those player piano things, she thought. Music would just float out of the piano—

Music began to float out of the piano. But it really was her playing. She stared bug-eyed at her fingers as they moved fluidly across the keys. What she was playing, she had no idea. It certainly wasn't the melody she'd tapped out all morning. But she recognized it from somewhere . . . yes. It was from a perfume commercial on television. This impossibly gorgeous model danced through a field of flowers while an impossibly gorgeous guy in a tuxedo chased her, and this music played.

Ms. Zooms ran back into the room. "You are playing, you do remember!"

Nicole stopped. "I really wanted that perfume."

"What perfume?"

Nicole sighed. "Never mind."

"Oh, my darling child." Before Nicole could stop her, Ms. Zooms was embracing her. "It's Beethoven's *Für Elise*. It is so beautiful. Beethoven was a wonderful German, not like the horrid Huns out there."

Being pressed to Bazooms' bazooms? This was over the top. Nicole closed her eyes. Please, please, please, she prayed. I don't care what this is, please let me go back to my real life. She opened them. Ms. Zooms was still squishing her.

"I brought some of your journals, Nicole. There are programs inside from your recitals. I thought perhaps it might trigger your memory to see them." She handed Nicole several thick notebooks bulging with newspaper and magazine clippings. "Look through them while I boil our rutabaga for supper."

"Rutabaga?" Nicole made a face.

"Yes, rutabaga."

Nicole saw Zooms' anxious expression. "I know this can't be fun for you," she acknowledged. "I'm sorry."

"Read the notebooks, Nicole, before your friends come

over." Ms. Zooms nodded quickly, then, as if to hide her emotions, took off for the kitchen. Nicole moved to the couch, plopped down, and put her feet up. She might as well be comfortable. She opened the notebook that had 1940 written on it to a random page. It was dated 20 October 1940. The handwriting was undeniably her own.

Today is the date by which all Jews in Paris must have registered with the French police. There are no exceptions. Posters all over Paris declare this. When Mimi and I walked home from school today, we must have passed at least ten of these posters.

When Papa came home from the hospital, he and Maman had another discussion about whether to register with the police. Maman was saying that we had no choice but to follow the Nazis' rules, and Papa was saying that he did not like the idea of the Nazis having a list of all the Jews of Paris. Maman asked him what did he want to do, run away from Paris and leave his patients in the hands of imbeciles? And what would happen if the Nazis took away our food ration cards because we did not register? In the end, Papa agreed to register us.

Nicole stopped reading. This was so bizarre. She flipped the pages toward the front. Throughout, it was definitely her handwriting.

Today is the blackest day Paris has ever known. The Nazis were marching in the city. I rode around on my bicycle and I shall never forget what I saw: columns of German soldiers, with their tanks and armored vehicles, their artillery and their supply wagons. Their uniforms gleamed. People stood and watched, awestruck. Already I saw French girls who speak German and German soldiers who speak French talking and flirting. You would never think that for the last six weeks tens of thousands of our soldiers have died fighting them. I admit, there was a moment or two today when I wished we had gone to Toulouse or to the countryside, but I know that Papa must stay at the hospital. When I came home, Maman was angry that I took my bicycle without asking her permission. But I am glad that I did it.

Nicole turned the page.

18 June 1940

Today I saw Adolf Hitler with my own eyes. He was sightseeing in my beloved city like any other tourist might. He stopped on the esplanade at the Palais de Chaillot. Mimi and I were riding our bicycles and we saw him there, surrounded by Boche swine, admiring the view of the Eiffel Tower. He had the proudest

look on his face. It made me want to retch. This
evening on the BBC we heard a broadcast from
London of a French general named de Gaulle urging
France not to give up the fight against the Germans. I
asked Papa if he knew who de Gaulle was, and he
just shook his head.

Dazed, Nicole put the notebook down. She picked up the next one, dated 1941. Sheets of paper fell out—newspaper clippings, movie advertisements, and the like. One was a handwritten playbill for a piano recital featuring Mme. Goldsteyn's students. Nicole looked at it closely. The third student scheduled to play was Nicole Bernhardt.

She picked up the movie advertisements. The titles were unfamiliar, and so were the stars: Viviane Romance, Albert Préjean, Danielle Darrieux. On one of them, she had crossed out Danielle Darrieux's name and scrawled Nazi swastikas all over it, along with the word *collabo.*

Collabo? What was that? From the swastikas she guessed that it wasn't a compliment. As she looked through more of the clippings, there was an enthusiastic knock on the front door.

"Take my key and please answer," Ms. Zooms called from the kitchen. "It's your friends."

More knocking, louder. Nicole put the journals and papers on the coffee table, got the key, and went to open the door. "This is just a dream. A really terrible dream."

She opened the door. Standing outside was Jack Polin.

"Nicole!" he exclaimed, and wrapped his arms around her. "I was so worried about you."

"On the other hand, I've had worse dreams." Nicole smiled wildly, as he held her at arm's length.

"What are you saying about dreams?"

"This is all just a little confusing. Uh, what are you doing here?"

His eyes searched hers. "Please say you remember me, Nicole."

"Well, yeah, but—"

"You *must* remember me. After all, I've been in love with you since the third grade."

nine

Y̶ou?" Nicole asked incredulously. "In love with me?"

Jack laughed. "You say it like it is news to you."

"It is."

"Very funny, Nicole," said someone standing behind Jack.

Nicole peered around him. "Mimi! I'm so glad to see you!" She hugged her friend. "Are you okay?"

"Of course I'm okay, you nut."

"But at the museum you—"

"Nico, I'm fine." Mimi kissed Nicole on both cheeks and sailed into the living room, Little Bit and Jack trailing in her wake.

"Now you see what I mean," Little Bit told them.

Jack took Nicole's hand. "Your sister said that as of this morning you still had not recovered your memory. Are you feeling any better now?"

Nicole gazed into his eyes. "Better and better all the time." Her fingers were entwined with his and he was looking at her the way she had always dreamed he would.

"Are you going to kiss her now?" Little Bit asked.

"Perhaps," Jack teased.

"What a great idea!" Nicole exclaimed.

Little Bit made a face. "That would be extremely disgusting. As well as immature."

"You know, Little Bit, this part of my dream would have been too perfect without you."

"*Little Bit?*" Jack echoed. "As in, a small morsel?"

Little Bit shrugged. "Right after she hit her head, she started calling me Little Bit."

"Liz-Bette?" Ms. Zooms appeared in the kitchen doorway. "Please leave Nicole alone with her friends and come set the table. Hello, Jacques, Mimi."

"Madame Bernhardt? We brought you a present." Mimi handed Ms. Zooms a cloth sack. "It is from our uncle's farm."

"Oh, thank you, Mimi." Ms. Zooms peered eagerly into the bag. "Vegetables. Tomatoes, zucchini, peppers. And cheese. How I love fresh cheese. I could eat an entire wheel of it by myself."

"No offense, Ms. Zooms," Nicole said, "but you could stand to lose a few el-bees. Do you know how many fat grams there are in cheese?"

"El-bees?" Mimi echoed.

"Dear God, my daughter has lost her mind."

"Bazooms, for the zillionth time, you have to stop calling me your daughter."

"Bah-Zooms?" Jack asked.

"She calls me Bah-Zooms," the older woman explained. "I have no idea what this means."

"I am going to call you Bah-Zooms, too," Little Bit declared.

"Enough rudeness, young lady. Come help me."

"But, Bah-Zooms, I want to stay here."

Mimi tugged on one of Little Bit's braids. "Come, Liz-Bette, I will help, too. Bye, Jacques, bye, Nicole. Have fun." She winked mischievously at them over her shoulder.

Nicole couldn't stop grinning. "Jack Polin," she marveled. "Alone with me. On purpose."

"*Jacques Poulin*," he corrected, making the *J* soft and changing the pronunciation of his last name. He sat on the couch and beckoned for Nicole to join him. "Do you think this is a Hollywood movie and I am some American movie star named Jack?"

Nicole laughed. "Works for me."

"Mimi and I have been so worried. Your mother saw our mother last evening and told her that you'd hit your head. I wanted to ring you, but since you don't—"

"Hold it." Nicole held her palm up. "Are you telling me that you and Mimi have *the same parents*?"

"It is usual for twins, don't you think?"

"You're *twins*?"

"I was born four minutes ahead of her, which is why I am smarter and better looking." He looked at Nicole expectantly, then frowned. "That is what I always say to make Mimi mad. You really don't remember?" Nicole shook her head.

He gently pushed some hair off her face. "When I heard

that you were hurt, my first thought was that you'd been arrested and roughed up. I was so worried. You take far too many chances, Nicole. You go out without your star—"

"I do?"

"You know you do. It is a foolish risk. Do you want to go to Drancy?"

"What's Drancy?"

"The detainment camp outside Paris."

She shrugged.

"It is the concussion," Jack said sympathetically. "You don't remember the Jewish regulations? Any of them?"

Nicole shook her head so blithely that Jack grabbed her by the shoulders.

"Listen, Nicole. You must relearn all the race laws for the Jews. It is extremely important. You cannot go outside after eight P.M. No radios, no bicycles, no telephones, no—"

"Hold on," Nicole protested. "What about you?"

"Me? I am not Jewish."

"Well, neither am I."

Jack's face darkened. "Nicole, you may *think* you are not Jewish because of your accident, but the Nazis and French police know that you *are* Jewish. Your father registered your family. It is stamped on your identity card. And it would not matter if you became Catholic tomorrow, because you have more than two Jewish grandparents and that is what the law calls a Jew. Therefore, you must act as if you are Jewish no matter what you think. Do you understand me? Do not leave this apartment again until all the rules are clear and you are prepared to obey them."

"Whatever you say, Jack," she joked. "I mean, Jacques."

"It is no joke, Nicole." He regarded her pensively. "If I asked you to do something for me, if it was very important, would you do it?"

"Honestly? Yes. I'd do pretty much anything," she confessed.

"Until your memory returns, I am begging you to call your family and your friends by their proper names. A mistake at the wrong time could draw attention to yourself. These days, that is something you do not want to do."

"No way am I calling Ms. Zooms *Maman*," Nicole protested. "I have a perfectly good *maman* who is making a fortune in real estate."

"Nicole, please. This is not funny. I love you. I want you to promise."

Everything in Nicole resisted. But this was Jack, the boy she had loved forever and who now pledged his love for her.

"All right," she said grudgingly. "Nicole Bernhardt, Mme. Renée Bernhardt, Dr. Jean Bernhardt, and the consistently annoying Liz-Bette Bernhardt. How's that?"

"Thank you." He glanced toward the kitchen. When he saw that no one was in the hallway, he turned back to her again, a sly glint in his eyes. "If you really do not remember anything, then if I kissed you right now, would it be as if we were kissing for the very first time?"

"Yes. But I'm a quick study." She closed her eyes and lifted her chin. Finally, it was really going to happen.

His lips met hers. Whatever world she was in didn't matter anymore, because there was nothing except this moment and this boy and this perfect kiss—

"That is disgusting!" Liz-Bette shrieked from the hallway. Nicole and Jacques flew apart, embarrassed.

"There you are, Liz-Bette," Mimi declared, rushing into the hallway. "Were you spying on them?"

"They were kissing. With spit."

"Liz-Bette, come here this moment!" Mme. Bernhardt's voice thundered from the kitchen.

"Everyone is always ordering me around." Liz-Bette pouted, but she obediently trudged away.

Mimi watched her go, then waltzed into the room. "Apologies for that unplanned interruption of your romantic interlude. But you didn't tell me, Nicole. What do you think of my star of solidarity?" She hit a modeling pose. Pinned to her blouse was a six-cornered yellow star like the one Nicole had worn the day before. But unlike Nicole's star, Mimi's was festooned with gaudy beads, sequins, and glitter.

"I see you added a typical Mimi touch," Nicole said. "Frankly, it's quite the fashion risk. So how come you're Jewish if Jack—I mean Jacques—isn't?"

"I'm not Jewish, and it's illegal to wear a star if you are not. That's why it's a political risk, you see," Mimi said proudly. "Some of us are brave enough to defy the lousy Huns and show our solidarity with you."

Nicole peered at Mimi's star again. There was hand-lettering in the center. "What's G-O-Y?"

"*Goy*," Jacques replied. "Yiddish for someone who is not Jewish."

"Yiddish?"

"The language of many refugee Jews," Mimi explained. "This is very bizarre, Nicole, your not remembering anything."

"I totally agree with you."

"Promise me you won't walk home with that thing on, Mimi," Jacques said.

"Oh, you," she scoffed, then strode to the window and looked out. "It's so strange. It still looks like the Paris I love, but it has been taken over by maniacs. I hate the Boche!"

"Why not just shout it out so all of Paris can hear?" Jacques asked sarcastically.

Mimi shot him a defiant look. "I wish I was in the Resistance."

"Very smart, Mimi. Our brother is a cop and you want to be in the Resistance."

"André is a French cop, not a Nazi."

Jacques threw his hands up in disgust. "He has to work with the Boche, doesn't he?"

"Well, he shouldn't," Mimi insisted. "He works for Pétain the imbecile and that madman Laval; they're both in the Nazis' pockets."

Nicole didn't understand. Who was Pétain? And Laval? She closed her eyes and pressed her fingers against her temples. The whole thing just made her headache come back.

"Nicole? Did you hear me?" Mimi asked.

"What? No, sorry."

"I said that unfortunately we have to leave because Maman gets nervous these days if we are not home early."

"Because of your foolishness," Jacques chided.

Mimi rolled her eyes. "I don't know how you can stand him, Nicole."

Nicole walked them to the door. Mimi kissed her on both cheeks, then went downstairs first so that Jacques could say good-bye to her alone.

"Do not misunderstand. I detest the Germans, too," Jacques told her. "I just want to keep my sister safe. And you. Your mother told me before that it is fine for you to go to school tomorrow so long as you stay with us. Mimi and I will meet you downstairs in the morning and we can walk together."

"School?" Nicole groaned.

"Just the other day you were telling me how glad you are that the Nazis still allowed Jews to go to school."

"Now, that *had* to be someone else."

"Stay safe, Nicole, I'll see you tomorrow," he whispered. He gave her the softest, sweetest kiss. Then, like a dream, he was gone.

ten

Nicole sat cross-legged on her bed, the journals Mme. Bernhardt had brought her that afternoon spread atop the bedspread. It was torture without a computer, because she really wanted to write. On her desk, along with her school-books, was an old-fashioned fountain pen and an inkwell. Well, it wasn't like she had a choice. She figured out how to fill the strange pen with ink, opened the 1942 journal to a blank page, and sat down to write.

June 15, 1942

Frightening Thought du Jour: *Sometimes when you're dreaming, it feels real. But if you're trapped in a dream—really trapped—how do you know if you're really dreaming at all?*

Welcome to My Nightmare:
   a. *My name is supposedly Nicole Bernhardt.*
   b. *It is no longer now. It's 1942.*
   c. *I was born and raised in Paris. My family is*

French on both sides for many generations. We live
in the sixteenth district at 8, avenue de Camoëns.
    d. I'm Jewish.

The Good, the Bad, the Ugly:
    a. The Good: *M is here. So is J, the boy I love who*
barely knows I exist. Only here he loves me and he
kissed me. Let's go to the videotape. Oh, yeah. HE
KISSED ME.
    b. The Bad: *The Nazis are here. They hate Jews so*
much that they don't even consider them people;
also, they want to take over the entire world. Even in
a dream, it's very scary.
    c. The Ugly: *My so-called father looks like my*
principal, Urkin. He's one of the few Jews still
allowed to practice medicine and is a doctor at the
Rothschild Hospital. He also has an office upstairs
from our apartment, where he writes. And my so-
called mother looks like my English teacher, Zooms.

∽

Nicole took one last look in the mirror over her mahogany
dresser. She'd brushed her hair with the silver-handled hair-
brush and selected an outfit from the closet. She knew vin-
tage stores that would pay a mint for all that retro chic. The
gray sweater she found was cashmere, with delicate pearl
buttons. She loved it. But all the skirts were calf-length, and
the ugly shoes with white socks? Excruciating.

At breakfast that morning, a friend of her father's, Dr. Windisch—a brain specialist no longer permitted to practice medicine—had come by to examine her. Dr. Windisch had declared her to be fine in the physical sense, which Nicole was happy to hear. But he'd frowned when she'd told him that she was a twenty-first century American. And definitely not Jewish.

"It's a curious case," Dr. Windisch had mused. "The best thing is to send her back into her normal routine and wait for her memories to return. They inevitably do."

Nicole gave her hair one last swipe with the brush, grabbed her books, and headed for the living room. "At least you look exactly like my daughter," Ms. Zooms teased when she walked into the living room. No, not Ms. Zooms. Mme. Bernhardt. Maman. She'd promised Jacques.

They walked downstairs and out into the sunshine to wait for Jacques and Mimi. So what if she was still stuck in the dream? It was a glorious morning. The boy she loved was on his way over to meet her. How bad could things be, really?

"Now, Nicole, remember. I have written your name and address on a scrap of paper and put it in your left shoe," Mme. Bernhardt said. "If you forget where you live—"

"I won't," Nicole interrupted gently, touched by the obvious depth of concern for her welfare. "I remember yesterday and the day before just fine. It's only before that . . ."

Mme. Bernhardt sighed. "Yes. Before that."

"Nicole!"

David Berg, clad in truly geeky knickers, was coming toward her. He had the same handsome face she remembered, and the same serious look in his eyes.

"David Berg!" she said happily. "Or is your name different here like everyone else's?"

"David Ginsburg," he corrected, removing his cap. "You know that."

"Hello, David," Mme. Bernhardt said. "Are you well?"

David nodded respectfully. "I heard you hit your head, Nicole."

Nicole shrugged. "So they tell me."

"Are you all right now?"

"Sure," Nicole said breezily.

David turned to Mme. Bernhardt. "May I talk to Nicole for a moment? Privately?"

"Of course. I will be just inside until you are finished." She went into the front hall of the building.

David edged toward the stone staircase a few feet away and motioned for Nicole to follow. She did. He looked very nervous. "I have to talk to you, Nicole."

"Yeah, sure. What's up?"

He gave her a sharp look. "How can you even ask me that? I came to say good-bye."

"But Mimi and Jacques are on their way over. You can walk to school with us."

"I'm not going to school, Nicole."

"Why? Where are you going?"

"I have word that soon—I don't know when, exactly—there is going to be a big roundup of foreign-born Jews."

He looked so sad. "Don't worry. None of this is real, David," she assured him. "I'm dreaming it all up."

"The whole world is in on it, then." And the whole world has gone insane." The intensity with which he spoke raised the hairs on her arms. "My family is going into hiding."

"Amazing. Like Anne Frank."

"Who is Anne Frank?"

"She lived in Amsterdam during—it's not important. Is there anything I can do to help you?"

He looked down at his worn shoes. "At first I told myself not to come tell you . . . what I'm about to tell you, because I would look so stupid. But then I thought, What difference could it possibly make anymore?"

"To tell me what?"

He wouldn't look at her. "Jacques always says that he has loved you since the third grade. And I . . . share his feelings."

She was touched. "You do?"

"I only want to say this to you, Nicole." He raised his eyes to hers. "Wherever I go, whatever happens to me . . . when I close my eyes, I will still see your face." He reached up and ripped the yellow star from his vest, stuffed it into Nicole's hand, and bolted down the stone staircase.

eleven

July 15, 1942

Mimi ran ahead down the rue de Passy. "I'm free-eee!" she cried, whirling around in a circle. "I think if I had to take even one more exam, I would scream."

Nicole caught up and linked arms with her. "You're already screaming," she pointed out nervously. "Everyone is staring at you."

"Let them stare, I don't care. I'm free-e-e!" As Mimi began whirling again, a passing older couple regarded her with disapproval.

"You're also insane," Nicole said. Mimi might not feel self-conscious on the street, but Mimi didn't have a yellow star sewn to her vest, either.

In the past month, Nicole had learned many things; from reading her journals, from family and friends, and from her own experience. It was hard living under the Occupation, but it was hardest of all if you were a Jew. Above all, you did not want to call attention to yourself.

They continued down the fashionable boulevard, idly looking into shop windows. They had walked this street together hundreds of times. Now, though, because of the Nazis' requisition of French goods for their war effort, there was little for the stores to display and even less for them to sell.

"Nicole, look at this." Mimi pointed to the window of a favorite boutique. Its single display mannequin wore a beautiful silk outfit, topped by an oversized, elaborate black-and-white hat. "Incredible," Mimi breathed, her face pressed to the glass. "What do you think, Nico?"

Nicole shrugged. "I think the dress is for show and not for sale. And if it was for sale, only the Nazis and their friends could afford it."

"I suppose," Mimi agreed reluctantly. "The hat is nice, though."

"Not worth the ration coupons. Come on." Nicole gently tugged Mimi away from the window.

"When this stupid war is over, I am going to be the best-dressed girl in Paris," Mimi vowed. "I'll never wear the same clothes twice. Instead of washing them, I'll toss them away like the Americans do."

Nicole laughed. "Americans don't do that."

Mimi rolled her eyes. "Oh, that's right. You still think you were an American and that you—"

"Lived in the future," they said at the same time.

"Nico, I admit I take pride in my own flights of fancy. But that dream of yours was the most bizarre thing ever."

Nicole bit her lower lip. "Sometimes I don't think it was a dream. Even now."

"What an imagination. You should become a science-fiction writer. *I Was a Twenty-First Century American*—what was it you called your dance group again?"

"Fly Girls," Nicole replied, feeling ridiculous.

"Exactly! *I Was a Twenty-First Century American Insect Girl*, by Nicole Judith Bernhardt, as recorded in her Paris journal on 15 July 1942."

"But it felt so real to me."

Mimi raised her eyebrows. "I don't know what dances better, your legs or your imagination."

Dancing. In a dizzying flash, one of the crazy visions came to Nicole again. Throbbing, manic music. Instead of singing, someone was shouting rhythmic poetry over it. She was wearing a black stretchy top that bared her stomach, and—

"Nicole, look." Mimi nudged her. Mimi's voice seemed very far away.

"What?" she asked faintly.

Mimi cocked her head at a stout middle-aged woman across the street. She carried a mesh shopping bag and sported the same fancy hat they had seen in the shop window. But the hat was far too large for her head, so it tilted over one eye at a precarious angle. Mimi laughed. "I see the latest Paris fashion didn't come in her size."

Nicole shook her head to clear it. The bizarre vision was gone. "You see, Mimi, if you bought the hat, that is how you would look."

Mimi leaned conspiratorially toward Nicole. "I could make three brassieres in my size with the material in that hat." She looked down at her flat chest and sighed. "Not that I need even one."

The woman crossed toward their side of the street, dodging bicyclists—since every drop of fuel was now powering Nazi tanks on the Russian front, cars had largely been replaced by bicycles—and made a beeline for a bakery that had a long queue in front of it. Her sour face grew even more unpleasant as she rummaged in her purse for her ration book, while the oversized hat teetered dangerously toward her nose. Watching her, Nicole and Mimi began to giggle uncontrollably.

The more they tried to compose themselves, the more they laughed. "Stop, stop. She'll know we're laughing at her," Nicole gasped. Just at that moment, a single potato fell from the woman's mesh bag. She stooped to pick it up and her hat toppled to the pavement. Then, more potatoes fell, one of them directly onto the hat's crown. The rest rolled into the street.

This was too much for Nicole and Mimi. They were convulsed with laughter all over again. "We have to stop! Think about something awful," Mimi instructed. "Pretend you just found out that Jacques is in love with another girl."

The thought sobered Nicole instantly. She would die if Jacques didn't love her anymore. In the American dream he didn't love her, and it was the worst thing in the world.

The hat lady gathered up all her potatoes and hurried toward the bakery. Nicole and Mimi edged close to the street to allow her to pass.

Only she didn't. Instead, she glared at the yellow star on Nicole's vest. Then she spit in Nicole's face. "Filthy Jew," she hissed, as the spit globule oozed down Nicole's left cheek. "It's because of Jew animals like you that sold us out that we're in this mess."

The woman strode away. Mimi quickly used her hand-kerchief to wipe Nicole's cheek. "She is a stupid collaborator cow." Shock and humiliation rendered Nicole mute.

"I cleaned it off, Nico. Forget the fat witch, eh? Come on. Let's go to Alain's cafe. Everyone will be waiting for us."

Nicole allowed Mimi to lead her down the street. They crossed the rue de la Tour, heading for the Cafe du Morvan. "Just think, Nicole," Mimi said, chattering to distract Nicole from what had just happened. "No more homework, just a whole summer of romantic possibilities. I am determined to get François to like me this summer. If I can just keep myself from talking about politics, I have a chance. You'll help me get him to notice me, won't you, Nico?"

"Wait," Nicole said, as they reached the cafe's front door.

"What?"

Nicole pointed to a large, hand-lettered poster affixed to the front door. FORBIDDEN TO JEWS.

A week before, the Nazis had issued another of their decrees against the Jews, barring Jews from going to cafes or restaurants. Nicole knew about the decree, but the Cafe du

Morvan had been her family's neighborhood cafe for years. In fact, a few days after the Nazi edict had gone into effect, M. Courot, the proprietor, had made a very public point of welcoming the Bernhardts in front of everyone, telling anyone who would listen that the Boche pigs were not going to decide who was welcome in his establishment.

But the FORBIDDEN TO JEWS sign hadn't been on the door then.

"Just take off your vest," Mimi suggested. Nicole still hung back. "I feel certain Alain would want you to. Come on, my idiot brother is in there."

Through the glass front of the cafe, Nicole saw Jacques sitting with Edouard, Suzanne, and Mimi's secret crush, François. Jacques's eyes caught Nicole's and he waved at her. She would do anything for him. Quickly, Nicole removed her vest and folded it with the star on the inside. They walked into the cafe. All their friends greeted them. Jacques put his arm around her. Nicole cuddled against him, feeling safe and loved.

Mimi slid into a seat next to handsome, dark-haired François, doing her best to look both casual and fetching.

"We were just talking about the Resistance," Jacques told Nicole. "They've struck again—a German supply train. They are so foolish to—"

"They are not foolish," Mimi interrupted sharply. "The resistants are heroes."

"Mimi is right," Suzanne agreed. "Someone has to stand up to Hitler. Listen to this." She grabbed a copy of a collaborationist newspaper someone had left on the next table. " 'For some days,' " she read, " 'Israelites, with or without their yellow stars, have with their continued insolence provoked a number of incidents in respectable cafes, hotels, and restaurants. The behavior of these Jews has been disgusting. But now, with General Oberg's order barring these creatures from nearly every public place where a true Frenchman would want to visit, peace and civility may reign when only disorder prevailed before.' Does anyone really believe this swill?"

Nicole's face reddened involuntarily. The "creatures" the newspaper spoke of were her and her family.

"So, what is it you propose to do?" Jacques asked. "Throw dirt clods at their tanks?"

"Whatever it takes," Mimi shot back defiantly.

"You should hear what else Oberg said, then." Jacques took the paper. " 'I have ascertained that it is the close friends and relatives of assailants, saboteurs, and troublemakers who have been helping them both before and after their crimes,' " he read. " 'I have therefore decided to inflict the severest penalties not only on the troublemakers, but on the families of these criminals.' "

"So?" Mimi challenged her brother. "Are you afraid?"

Jacques glanced at her coldly and read on. " 'One. All male relatives, including brothers-in-law and cousins over the age of eighteen, will be shot. Two. All females will be sentenced to hard labor. Three. All children of men and women affected by these measures will be put in reform schools—' "

90

"Here we go again," François groaned. "Politics, politics, politics. I am sick of hearing about politics."

Mimi turned on him. "How can you be? Imbecile Huns are running our country, and imbecile French are helping them!" Across the table, Nicole made a motion to Mimi to zip her lip, but she knew Mimi couldn't help herself.

"It is always the same thing," François groused, as he sipped his ersatz coffee. "I am not political. It bores me, really. I am *zazou*."

Nicole laughed. "You are not zazou. *They* are zazou." She pointed through the cafe window to a knot of young men and women who sat at an outdoor table.

The zazous was the name given to a movement of rebellious young people who disdained politics. They all went to the same cafes and listened to "swing" music. The messy, long-haired boys wore oversized jackets, the girls wore sweaters with huge shoulder pads, and they all wore sunglasses, even indoors.

"Where are your sunglasses, Monsieur Zazou?" Suzanne teased François. "Where is your long, greasy hair?"

François blushed. "It is not my fault that I am forced to live under the domination of my narrow-minded parents."

Suzanne laughed and leaned over to kiss his cheek. "It's all right, François. I understand. You are zazou on the inside."

Everyone laughed, even François, because there was something so sweet about Suzanne that even he could not take offense. Nicole thought about how pretty and nice she was, and how her heart had been shattered when Jacques had confessed that he loved her, because—

No. That didn't happen. That was the American dream. Mostly, Nicole knew that now. But there still were flashes that felt so real— No. Jacques did not love Suzanne. He loved her. Only her. Forever. She snuggled closer to him, and he smiled.

"Where's the waiter?" he wondered aloud. "I want to order you the best national coffee in Paris."

Nicole made a face. National coffee, made from ground roots and chicory, was a joke. There wasn't a single coffee bean in it.

"National coffee for everyone," François proposed grandly. "Forget politics. Let's swing like the Americans."

"Oh, I love swing!" Mimi exclaimed.

"Excellent." François leaned over and planted a comically huge smooch on Mimi's cheek; everyone began teasing them. Just then, M. Courot came out from the kitchen and hurried to their table.

"Nicole, I am terribly sorry, but you must leave."

"But she was here with me just a few days ago," Mimi protested. "You welcomed her then."

"I welcome her now," M. Courot said, his voice quavering. "But three Huns are checking my storeroom. Go, quickly. If they do an identity check they'll arrest you. Then they'll arrest me. Go!"

Nicole's heart pounded as she grabbed her vest and book

bag from the table. Mimi stood, followed by Jacques and Suzanne. "If you're leaving, we're leaving," Mimi insisted.

"Stay," Nicole said. "I have to get home anyway."

"I want to walk you home," Jacques declared.

"We all will," Mimi added.

"No. I'll see you tomorrow." She hurried toward the door without looking back.

twelve

It isn't fair.

Nicole passed the concierge's ground-floor apartment and ascended the beautiful circular staircase that led to her family's fourth-floor flat, wondering why things couldn't be like they used to be. Before the war, she had written in her journals that being Jewish had never made her feel different from her friends. Even in the American dream, as far as she could remember, Jews were treated the same as everyone else.

Now, everything had changed.

"Nicole, is that you?" her mother's anxious voice rang down the hall as Nicole pushed open the apartment door.

"No, it's Scarlett O'Hara," Nicole muttered under her breath, naming a character from a favorite American novel.

Mme. Bernhardt hurried to the door and embraced her. She wore an apron over a beautiful dove gray dress that was much too big. Funny. Nicole had hardly noticed before. Because there was so little to eat, even her plump mother was growing slender.

"Where were you?" Mme. Bernhardt asked sharply.

Nicole sighed. Why did her mother always sound as if she were interrogating her? "With Jacques and Mimi. The lift is stuck again, I had to walk up."

"I told you to come straight home from your exams, Nicole."

"Am I not even allowed to have a social life?"

Her mother smiled sadly. "Later on, I'm sure of it. But now, not so much of one."

Nicole looked away. Mme. Bernhardt put her hand to her daughter's chin and gently turned Nicole's face to hers. "Listen to me. I care more about your safety than I care about your fun. Do you understand me?"

"Yes, Maman."

"Good. I managed to get some beans. I cooked them with vermicelli for dinner."

"I'm not hungry." Nicole went to sit on the couch. Her mother followed, maternal antennae on full alert.

"Something happened today," she concluded.

A woman spit on me on the street, Maman.

"Nothing happened."

"Tell me."

M. Courot told me, in front of my friends, to leave the cafe. FORBIDDEN TO JEWS.

"I told you, nothing." Nicole jumped up. She couldn't bear just sitting there. "I'm going down to Claire's."

Mme. Bernhardt folded her arms. "You are telling now instead of asking, young lady?"

"*May* I go downstairs to Claire's?"

"Yes, you may." Her mother smoothed hair off her face. "Try not to take everything so hard, my child. The Occupation will not be forever."

"I'll try." She kissed her mother on each cheek, then headed for the door.

"Take your identity card," Mme. Bernhardt called.

"I'm only going—"

"Nicole . . ." Her mother's voice held an unspoken three-part warning, one that Nicole had heard voiced many times before.

It's always dangerous.

You must always carry your identity card.

You must always be careful because you are a Jewish girl.

Irritated, Nicole got her book bag. It contained the identity card that said that she was a French citizen and had the word *Jew* stamped on it in disgusting red letters. Then she ran down the two flights to the Einhorns' flat. At least going to Claire's meant going somewhere, which Nicole figured was better than staying locked up in her own flat like some kind of caged animal.

According to Mme. Bernhardt, she and Claire had once been good friends, but had drifted apart when Claire's parents sent her to a Jewish academy several years before. Nicole found Claire immature and unsophisticated, compared with her "real" friends. But at least Claire understood what it felt like to be singled out as a Jew.

Nicole knocked. Mme. Einhorn opened the door. Her thin face broke into a smile. The Einhorns' dog, an annoying toy poodle named Bon-Bon, began barking, jumping up and down with excitement.

"Down, Bon-Bon. Bad dog!" Mme. Einhorn scolded the dog, then kissed Nicole on each cheek. "You are a mind reader, my dear. Claire is in her bedroom feeling quite tragic. Even her bubbe can't joke her out of it. Go cheer her up. But say hello to Claire's bubbe first. You know how she loves you. She's in her room."

Claire's tiny Polish bubbe, which was Yiddish for grandmother, was so fond of Nicole that she had asked Nicole to call her Bubbe Einhorn. Since Bubbe Einhorn spoke only Polish and Yiddish, Claire had translated this request into French.

Nicole couldn't figure out why Bubbe Einhorn liked her, since they could barely communicate. Still, she dutifully stuck her head into Bubbe Einhorn's room. The old woman was sitting in a chair, knitting a sweater.

"Hello, Bubbe Einhorn."

"Hello, Nicoleh," Bubbe Einhorn responded fondly, smiling at Nicole. *Ze gut tsu zen a shayn maideleh.*

Nicole smiled and nodded. The only words she recognized were *shayn maideleh*, which meant *pretty girl* in Yiddish. Still, she nodded again politely, excused herself, and walked down to Claire's room, where she tapped on the door.

"Claire? It's Nico."

"Come in." Claire was lying on her bed, her thick red braids spilling onto her freckled arms.

"Your mother said you were feeling tragic." Nicole sat on the wooden chair at Claire's desk. "Me, too."

"I can't stand my mother." Claire scowled. "She's such a hypocrite. The world is falling apart but in front of me she pretends it isn't, as if I am a stupid child who must be protected from reality."

"My mother treats me like a child, too."

"Well, all I have to say is that when I am a mother I will respect my daughter's intelligence," Claire said. "Once she turns thirteen, I will allow her to make decisions for herself. Of course, I'll probably never get married because no boys even like me."

Usually Nicole tried to talk Claire out of her negativity, but today she didn't feel like it. She got up and wandered aimlessly around Claire's room. Her eyes lit on a magazine photo taped to the wall, of the American movie stars Ginger Rogers and Fred Astaire. Fred was dipping Ginger—her wavy blond hair almost brushed the floor.

Nicole touched the picture. "I wish I could go dancing."

"By the time they let us Jews go dancing again, we'll be too old to want to," Claire predicted.

Irritation crept up the back of Nicole's neck. "You always look at the dark side, Claire."

"I face facts." Claire examined the frizzy end of one braid.

"Everything is getting worse. There is one Nazi decree after another. And no decent food."

Why did Claire always go on like this? Nicole felt even more restless. She didn't want to be home but she didn't want to be here, either. Yet there was no place else she could be. She decided to go back upstairs and read. Maybe she'd reread *Gone with the Wind.* For quite a while, Scarlett O'Hara hadn't had any decent food to eat, either.

"I'll just be going . . ." Nicole started for the door.

"Don't leave!" Claire begged. "I thought you might want to stay for supper."

"No, I don't think so."

"Oh, come on. Whatever my mother prepared will be awful, so none of us will mind eating less. You could spend the night, too."

Nicole considered the offer. She couldn't go out with Jacques or Mimi because of the Jewish curfew. Being with Claire would be better than spending the night with her sister.

"My mother will want me to eat at home," Nicole decided. "She won't want me to share your rations. But I suppose I could come back down after."

"Wonderful!" Claire beamed. She jumped up and hugged Nicole.

Nicole felt guilty that she didn't like Claire nearly as much as Claire liked her. Why is it that people never love or like each other equally? she thought. There's always one who cares more. A terrible thought hit her stomach, so physical it felt as if she had been punched: I love Jacques more than he loves me.

"I'm so glad you're my best friend now," Claire said.

Nicole smiled to be polite. Really, though, she wasn't thinking about Claire at all. She was still thinking about Jacques, thoughts she would not dare confess to a living soul, not even to Mimi.

I can't go to cafes with Jacques, or to the movies or concerts or to the park, or anywhere, anymore. So why would Jacques want to be with me, anyway?

Why would he want to be with a Jew?

thirteen 13

They gathered around the radio in the Einhorns' living room and quietly hummed along to the familiar tones that opened the British Broadcasting Corporation's nightly short-wave radio transmission, *The French Speak to the French.* Nicole loved that the broadcast always began with the first notes of Beethoven's Fifth Symphony, as if the BBC was saying to the Nazis, "Look! Look how far you have fallen from the best of what is German." She also knew that the *dit-dit-dit-dah* of those four notes spelled out the letter *V* in Morse code: *V* for victory.

Listening to the London-based BBC was the only way for French people to get honest war news. All the French newspapers had been transformed into outlets for Nazi propaganda. So, though Jews were forbidden to have radios, both the Bernhardts and the Einhorns had decided to risk it.

"Move the antenna," Claire urged her mother. "I can hardly hear."

"Shhh!" her bubbe admonished, as Jean Oberle, the popular French voice of the BBC, began to speak. As he did,

Mme. Einhorn whispered a translation into Yiddish for her mother-in-law.

This is the BBC, London, 15 July 1942.
The news is being read by Jean Oberle.
In France, Royal Air Force planes swept over Brittany during the day and attacked a variety of military objectives. In Paris, five additional members of a French family have been sentenced to death for the killing of a German soldier by a member of that family, in accordance with the new regulations announced by General Oberg. And from the collaborationist regime at Vichy comes word that French colonial authorities may confiscate Jews' property anywhere in the colonies. In a new decree—

A burst of loud static interrupted the broadcast. "The lousy Huns are jamming the BBC again," Claire fumed.

"Don't say *lousy*," her mother corrected her, fiddling with the radio dial. All she got was more static.

Claire rolled her eyes as her mother searched for the signal without success. "Let's go to my room, Nicole." They said good night and went to look through some of Claire's old movie magazines. Then Claire wanted to plan the weddings they'd have one day, down to each morsel of food and drink that would be served—smoked salmon, roast chicken, champagne—food that hadn't been seen by ordinary Parisians in more than a year.

"My wedding gown will have to be fabulous since I'm so plain," Claire declared. "If I am ever able to convince a boy to marry me, he'll probably be homely."

"Claire Einhorn, you are the most negative person I know."

Claire pulled apart some split ends on one braid. "If I said I was going to marry the handsomest boy in Paris, you would find me ridiculous and I would find myself ridiculous. I prefer to be mature about it. Now, back to the food. Perhaps I would prefer roast duck to chicken."

They kept up their chatter even after Claire's mother came in to tell them to change for bed. Finally, Nicole told Claire to stop, it was making her too hungry. They both changed into their nightgowns. When Nicole reached into her book bag for her toothbrush, her journal slipped out.

Claire eyed it curiously. "What is that?"

"It's private." Nicole quickly stuffed the journal back into her bag.

"Best friends aren't supposed to keep secrets from each other, you know," Claire said.

You are not my best friend, Claire, Nicole longed to tell her. It took all her self-control not to do so. The two of them crawled into Claire's narrow bed as Claire's mother opened the door.

"All tucked in, girls?"

"Maman, I asked you to knock before you just barge in," Claire said imperiously.

"I'll try to remember," her mother said. She kissed them both good night. "Sweet dreams, you two." She closed the door softly behind her. Nicole turned over, trying to get comfortable.

"Nico?" Claire's voice was small.

"What?"

"Do you suppose we'll have our weddings in France?"

"Of course we will. Go to sleep."

"I'm not so sure. I heard my father telling my mother that we should have gone to England when we had the chance. But now it's too late."

Nicole rolled over and stared thoughtfully at the shadows on the ceiling. "That can't be right. America is in the war now, so it's just a matter of time. I imagine your father is simply a worrier like you, Claire. Where is he, anyway?"

"I'm not supposed to say."

"He shouldn't be out so late. He doesn't have an Ausweis."

The importance of a German Ausweis had been hammered home to Nicole by her parents. The official pass allowed the holder to be out after curfew and instructed any patrols to let the holder travel unhindered. It was more valuable to a Jew than gold. Nicole's father had been issued one because his hospital was under the auspices of the UGIF, the Union Generale des Israelites de France, the organization the Nazis had mandated for the Jews to administer Jewish affairs. Nicole and her family felt safer because of it.

Nicole studied Claire's profile. "Do you know how dangerous it is for him to be out?"

"Of course I do. Besides, he's not *out*, exactly. He's . . ." She turned to Nicole. "Do you promise not to tell?"

"I promise."

"Cross your heart and hope to die?"

"Claire, we're Jewish. We don't cross our hearts."

"It's just an expression, silly." Claire sat up. "I'm only telling because you're my best friend. My father is doing something top secret."

Nicole was shocked. She sat up, too. "You mean he's in the Resistance?"

"No. He's working on a musical composition."

"But where? Jews can't—"

"That's why it's a secret," Claire said impatiently. "He's rehearsing a famous string quartet in a flat near the Bastille. He stays in the crawl space up above the ceiling in case the Gestapo comes. My father lies on his stomach, listens, and speaks to them through a grate."

Nicole tried to imagine it. "Your father is very brave."

Claire shrugged. "He is an artist. He does what an artist must do."

Claire's words reverberated in Nicole's head. At that moment she liked Claire better than she had in a long, long time.

༄

Through her sleep's fog, Nicole heard her mother knocking on her door. She was sure her mother wanted her to do some awful chore, but Nicole just wanted to go back to the glorious dream she was having about Jacques. They were on vacation at the sea, eating fresh fruit and kissing on the sandy—

More knocking. Relentless! Her mother was just so demanding. There was no school today. What kind of chore was so important that she had to be awakened early?

"Let me sleep," she groaned.

A hand shook her roughly. "Nicole. Wake up!"

Claire's voice instantly snapped Nicole to consciousness.

"Someone is at the front door. I don't think my mother can hear." Her face was right next to Nicole's, her eyes huge. "What should we do?"

Bon-Bon started yapping at whoever was knocking. Nicole's heart thudded. "Go wake your mother, quickly."

"Do I have to?"

The knocking stopped, and the two girls held their breath. Then it began again, even louder, and Nicole pushed Claire off the bed. "Yes. Now, go!"

Claire ran. Nicole waited, hardly daring to move. The incessant knocking continued. Finally, Claire returned. "My mother said we're not to come out unless she tells us to," she reported breathlessly.

"Maybe it's nothing." Nicole was able to make out the clock on Claire's nightstand. It was five o'clock in the morning.

Shouting joined the pounding; Nicole and Claire could hear it through the closed door. "French police! Open the door, please."

Nicole nearly fainted with relief. "It's all right, they're not Gestapo, they're French." The girls peeked out from Claire's room as Mme. Einhorn opened the front door to the policemen.

"We must see the identity cards of everyone in the apartment, please," the taller, darker-haired cop said.

"My daughter and mother-in-law are sleeping," Mme. Einhorn said. "I don't want to wake them."

"Please wake them immediately," the shorter cop said. He had small eyes and a bulbous nose, as unattractive as the other was handsome. "They must present their identity cards."

"It's the middle of the night," Mme. Einhorn protested.

"Identity cards must be presented at once," the short cop insisted.

Claire shut the door and stared mutely at Nicole. Through the wall, they could hear Claire's mother speaking to her mother-in-law in Yiddish. Soon, Mme. Einhorn came into Claire's room. "It's all right," she assured the girls. "They are just doing an identity check."

Moments later, all four of them were at the front door, identity cards in hand. Bubbe Einhorn, wrapped in a beautiful shawl, looked boldly at the handsome cop as she handed over her card. The shorter cop checked something off on a file card he was holding. "Where is M. Einhorn?"

"He stayed the night with friends," Claire's mother explained smoothly. The policeman didn't react. He simply checked off something else, then pulled out a piece of paper and read from it.

" 'By order of the Prefecture of Police, you are being arrested.' " Claire gasped. The policeman continued. " 'All alien Jews of the following nationalities: German, Austrian, Polish—' "

"Excuse me, gentlemen." Mme. Einhorn roughly pushed Nicole forward. "This girl is not an alien Jew. Look again at her identity card, please. She is French, a neighbor, visiting us from the fourth floor."

The policeman shrugged. " 'All children living with the person or persons arrested shall be taken away with them, no member of the family shall remain behind in the apartment.' "

"But this girl does not live—"

"You will take your ration cards," the other cop interrupted. "You may each take no more than two suitcases. Inside, you may pack one pair of shoes, two pairs of socks, two blankets—"

"This girl lives upstairs," Mme. Einhorn pleaded. "She is French." She took Nicole by the shoulders and steered her toward the door. "Her father is a doctor at the—"

But the dark-haired cop stepped between Nicole and the door. "We have orders and a schedule to follow. We will sort out problems later. Quickly now, please. You may pack enough food for two days, one sweater, one drinking glass, one fork, one spoon—"

"You have ten minutes," the other cop added.

"Go, Claire, quickly, and collect your things," Mme. Einhorn told her petrified daughter. Then she explained everything to her mother-in-law in rapid Yiddish. The old woman gave the policemen a cold look before going to pack.

Nicole wanted to cry. Her own parents were so close, upstairs in their warm, safe beds. But crying would do no good. Instead, she gulped hard and addressed the taller of the two cops, because he was so handsome and had a kind voice.

"Excuse me, please," she began, trembling. "My father is Dr. Jean Bernhardt of the Rothschild Hospital, and—"

"You now have eight minutes," the tall cop said. His indifferent eyes met Nicole's. She had been mistaken. There was no kindness there at all.

Mme. Einhorn turned to Nicole. "Go to Claire's room. Pack some of her things for yourself. Hurry."

Nicole ran to Claire's room. Claire gave her a small valise and Nicole filled it with clothes, not bothering to look at what she was packing. Claire sat on her bed, sobbing and rocking Bon-Bon in her arms, a half-filled valise next to her.

"Stop sniveling and pack," Nicole ordered.

"Don't yell at me!"

Nicole took a deep breath to calm herself even as she filled the valise. "Pack as much as you can, Claire. You must do it now." After Nicole had filled her own valise, she helped Claire. Then she glanced at her book bag with the journal in it on the floor. She stuffed it into the valise as well.

When they gathered again by the front door, Claire was still sobbing and clutching Bon-Bon. "I have to take my dog."

"The dog must be left with your concierge," the shorter

cop said. "Follow quietly, please." They had no choice but to lug their valises down to the main floor of the building. Mme. Genet, the concierge, stood in the hall, her chin held self-righteously high. The short cop handed Bon-Bon to her.

"I don't want this beast," she protested.

"Just for a short while," Mme. Einhorn pleaded quietly, "until we return. For my little girl." Mme. Genet scowled, but took the animal.

"And you will please make sure the utilities are cut off in the flat," the shorter policeman instructed her.

"When will they be back?" Mme. Genet asked. Neither cop answered.

"Please, Madame Genet," Nicole said quickly. "Go tell my father that I've been arrested. He must come for me—"

"We must go now," the short cop said, opening the front door.

Nicole looked back at Mme. Genet. "Please. Tell him now!"

They dragged their suitcases outside. The cops led them toward the stone staircase. Nicole looked back again. Mme. Genet was still at the door, a small smile of satisfaction on her lips, Bon-Bon whimpering in her arms.

f o u r t e e n

July 16, 1942

They were held briefly at the local police precinct, where they learned their destination: the Vélodrome d'Hiver, the indoor bicycle arena known to everyone as the Vel d'Hiv. It was across the Seine, not more than twenty minutes on foot from Nicole's apartment.

Within a half-hour the cops were walking them and a group of other detainees to the Vel d'Hiv. Save for a bird chirping, Claire's snuffling, and the lonely footfalls of shoes against the pavement, Paris was silent. Nicole tried to assure herself that everything would be fine, that her father would rescue her. Over and over in her head, in time to her foot-falls: *I am French and Papa has an Ausweis, I am French and Papa has an Ausweis.* She wasn't as confident about what would happen to the Einhorns, though. She heard that some arrested Jews had been resettled in Poland. Others were held hostage by the Germans, to be executed in reprisal for acts of resistance. Maybe there was some way her father could rescue them, too.

Nicole looked at Claire, who continued to snuffle. "Don't

cry. Nothing bad will happen," she assured her, even though she didn't believe it herself.

"Liar." Claire blew her nose on her sleeve. "Will Mme. Genet take care of Bon-Bon, do you think?"

"I'm sure she will."

The police led them all across the bridge over the Seine and along the boulevard de Grenelle. Nicole looked up at the Eiffel Tower, shrouded in early-morning fog, as if hiding in shame from what was occurring on the streets below. When Nicole had been just a little girl, her father had explained that the tower was a symbol to the world of the splendor of Paris.

Funny, Nicole thought. No, peculiar. This was the first time since her accident that she'd remembered something from her French childhood without prompting from her parents or her journals.

She switched her valise from hand to hand as they walked past a few shopkeepers preparing to open. The shopkeepers glanced at them diffidently. The Vel d'Hiv was coming into view. Though used now mostly for fascist political rallies, she recalled going there with her father to watch bicycle races on a banked oval track. She could picture herself on her father's shoulders, both of them laughing, cheering for their favorite racer.

It was the strangest feeling—memories seemed to be rushing at her.

Outside the Vel, the rue Nelaton was a sea of hundreds of well-guarded Jews. The prisoners carried cloth-wrapped bundles or suitcases. Some women wheeled baby carriages piled with blankets and clothing. Green-and-gray municipal buses were pulling up, children's wide-eyed faces pressed up against the windows.

"They're going to kill us," Claire said, her voice low.

"Stop being so melodramatic," Nicole snapped. "This is France. No one is killing anyone." She and the Einhorns joined a long queue that led to a police checkpoint. Across the street, a Catholic priest walked by on his way to early-morning mass. A woman broke from their queue, ran across the street, and threw herself at the priest's feet, begging him to save her children.

"Don't look," Mme. Einhorn instructed. "That poor woman is mentally deranged. We are all going to be fine."

Too late. Nicole and Claire were already looking. "Help us!" the woman pleaded, loud enough for the crowd to hear. "They took a hundred Jews from my building alone. You cannot look the other way, you are a man of God!" The terror-stricken priest extricated himself from her arms and hurried away.

They waited and waited as the line slowly snaked forward. "This way please, madame," a pock-faced cop told a young mother near them. She held a large valise in one arm and a baby in the other. Two more children clutched at her skirt. She shifted the weight of the baby and stumbled, dropping her valise. Wordlessly, the cop picked it up. Silent tears streaked his face. Nicole stared in awe. It was the first time she had ever seen a policeman cry.

Finally, after the crowd had grown to thousands, Nicole and the Einhorns reached the French officials who were checking identity cards against long lists of names.

Mme. Einhorn grabbed Nicole's arm. "This is your chance, tell them who you are."

"But what about you?"

"We'll be fine, just do it," she insisted.

Nicole addressed the official behind the table. "Excuse me, monsieur, but this is a mistake." Her voice quavered as she handed him her identity card. "I'm French as you can see, my father is—"

"Into the Vel you go. Next." He pushed Nicole's card back at her, his eyes already on the next person in line. If he had heard what she said, he didn't care.

After all, she was just another Jew.

∽

Nicole was awake, but her eyes were closed. The self-imposed darkness made everything a bit more tolerable.

"I can't breathe," Claire complained. "Can you, Nicole?"

Reluctantly, Nicole opened her eyes. Claire was wiping her sweaty forehead. "Talk less, you'll breathe better."

Claire pouted. "That's stupid. Nothing will keep me cool. We're all going to suffocate to death. Why won't they give us water?"

Nicole fought the urge to slap Claire's face. Didn't Claire realize that they were all as miserable as she was? Couldn't she stop complaining?

They had been in the arena for six hours, sitting in the second row of seats above the central floor area. All the Jews outside had been forced inside; more arrived all the time through the main doors to their left. Many of the new arrivals were children. Families staked out living areas wherever they could still find space—in the aisles, in the bleachers, anywhere.

How could this be happening, Nicole wondered. The Nazis were barbarians, everyone knew that. It was one thing for atrocities to take place in little villages in Poland or on the Russian front. But here? In Paris? In the most sophisticated city in the world? With the cooperation of French police?

In the last six hours she'd seen terrible things—old people rocking themselves like babies, babies listless from dehydration with the dull stare of the old. One shrieking woman had been taken away by the police, who made a point of saying that she was faking insanity but that her "Jewish trick" wouldn't work.

Worst of all was the mother who had begged the police to help her vomiting child. They did nothing. Now, Nicole looked over at the little girl, who lay still on the floor, her eyes rolled back in her head.

Occasionally there were announcements over the public address system, such as where to go for medical treatment. But Nicole knew that if treatment were actually available, the sick child would be under a doctor's care.

"Attention, attention," a deep voice boomed over the

loudspeaker. "In the event of an unexpected death, bring the body to area two hundred on the main level. I repeat, in the event of an unexpected death, bring the body to area two hundred on the main level."

"Maman?" Claire asked, her voice trembling, when she heard the announcement.

"It's nothing," her mother assured her. "Only for those who were brought here gravely ill."

"If they don't give us water we'll all be gravely ill."

Nicole willed herself to block out Claire's voice. She didn't want to think about water. Or food. Earlier, Mme. Einhorn had offered them some cold rutabaga. But Nicole hadn't eaten, figuring that food would only make her more desperate for a toilet than she already was. And toilets were an impossibility. The vast majority of them were locked so no one could try to escape through the washroom windows. By mid-morning, word had spread that the only two functioning commodes were jammed.

Jammed or not, people were still queuing up to use them. So far Nicole had resisted the urge. But Claire's words had put her over the edge. "I'll be back," she told the Einhorns.

"Bring us back pastries and coffee," Mme. Einhorn said with an ironic smile. "I'll tip you well." Nicole wanted to smile, too, but couldn't manage it. Instead, she went to join the line for the stopped-up toilets.

fifteen

W e'll never get in."

Nicole looked behind her. The statement had come from a young woman holding a diapered baby who was next in line. "We will, eventually," Nicole replied, hoping against hope that the line would move more quickly. If she didn't reach the toilet soon, she thought she would explode.

"A man over there had the right idea," the young mother said, cocking her head toward the other side of the Vel. "He jumped off the highest tier of seats."

"Is he—?"

"Dead? Yes. Lucky bastard." Her baby began to fuss. "This is Daniel. Today is his first birthday."

Daniel moaned, then loudly fouled his diaper, adding to the stench from the bathrooms. Nicole clasped her hand to her mouth, sure she was going to vomit. The toilet would have to wait. She stepped out of line and hurried away. As she headed back toward the Einhorns, she passed women who were squatting to relieve themselves along the walls,

117

hiding their faces in shame. She would never, *ever* do that, she vowed, no matter what.

When she returned, Claire was asleep, her head in her grandmother's lap. For some reason, Mme. Einhorn was staring intently at the main gate.

Nicole tried to find ways to distract herself. She made a halfhearted effort to write in her journal, but found it impossible. It was too noisy—how could anyone concentrate? Then she invented a mental game, weaving stories about new people as they arrived. A beautiful flaxen-haired girl, who looked to be just a little older than she, caught Nicole's attention. She wore a lovely blue dress with pearl buttons, and a matching ribbon held back her long hair.

She comes from a poor but noble family, Nicole invented. An older rich man—an aristocrat!—fell in love with her and showered her with gifts, like the expensive outfit she's wearing. But the aristocrat was caught working with the Resistance and now the girl has no one to protect her.

Suddenly, the beautiful girl looked directly at Nicole. Nicole smiled, hoping that she might make a friend. But the girl turned away. After a while, Nicole saw her join the line for the broken toilets.

Nicole got bored with her game and nodded off. Sometime later, Claire's voice woke her. "Maman, I can't hold it anymore."

Instead of answering, Mme. Einhorn opened her valise and dug for the old newspapers that lined the bottom.

"What are you doing?" Claire asked, as her mother spread the newspapers out on the floor.

"There, Claire," she told her daughter. "Here is your bathroom. I will hold a sheet up for you, for privacy. It is a collaborationist paper, so it will hide the truth very well."

Claire looked aghast. "I can't do that."

"You can, and you will."

"No, I can't. It's disgusting!"

Bubbe Einhorn muttered something in Yiddish and tottered over to the newspaper where Mme. Einhorn held the sheet in front of her. "You see? Your bubbe is going first."

Finally, Claire eased herself behind the sheet. Nicole turned away and managed to sink back into the safety of sleep.

ᔆ

Hours later, she awoke with a throbbing headache. The Vel was hotter and even more crowded; her parched lips stuck to her teeth. Her whole body ached for a toilet.

No. She would not squat on newspaper like some kind of paper-trained pet. She looked around, hoping to distract herself from the discomfort. The beautiful flaxen-haired girl had returned, with an older woman. Her mother? The girl was in tears, trying to wipe feces off her mother's legs with a piece of underwear. Blood ran down the girl's bare legs, and Nicole realized with horror that she was menstruating and had no sanitary napkins to stop the flow.

The girl saw Nicole eyeing her; Nicole looked away. Pretend dignity, she figured, was better than no dignity at all. Then several infants began bawling; Nicole put her hands over her ears and closed her eyes to block out the din. If only her mind could carry her away. She tried to conjure up her American life—or dream—or whatever it was. It was the future. And . . . was there to be some sort of show? Where she would dance? Yes. She would wear a skirt as short as a toddler's pinafore. Her friends would be there. Oh, there would be food! She could almost taste it. Small, round candies in different colors, with hard candy shells and chocolate inside that melted in your mouth. Bowls of crisp potato slices, so thin that you could almost see through them. You'd pop a whole handful into your mouth and lick the salt off your fingers, and—

"Nicole?"

Claire tugged at her sleeve. No. She refused to hear, wanting to stay in the world of the future. But when she tried to imagine the scene again, it looked like a photo someone had thrown into the fire; the edges curling, burning, disappearing to ash.

"Nicole?" Claire repeated. Nicole opened her eyes.

"What?"

"Do you hate me?"

"Why would I hate you?"

"If you hadn't been at my flat, you wouldn't be here now. I know you didn't really want to stay. I'm sorry."

Nicole felt a stab of guilt. "It's not your fault. I don't blame you."

"I know you only started being friends with me again because I live in your building and I'm Jewish."

"No, I—"

"It's all right," Claire said, her plain, freckled face solemn. "I know it's true. You don't have to deny it. I want you to know I don't blame you, either."

Mme. Einhorn moved closer to her daughter. When she spoke, her voice was low, her eyes glued to the front entrance. "Claire, listen to me. You are going to escape."

Claire sat up, her eyes wide. "No, I—"

"Yes," her mother insisted. "I have been watching. The guards are all French. I do not believe they would shoot to kill. We will watch, and when the guards change shifts, Bubbe and I will create a commotion. Then, Claire, you will slip past the guards and run. Go to— Come here."

"I don't want to do this. Don't make me."

"This is not an issue for discussion. Your papa and I have prepared for this possibility."

"No."

Mme. Einhorn harshly pulled her daughter to her and whispered in her ear. Then she held her at arm's length. "Do you understand, Claire? Go there. Do not stop to speak to anyone."

"No, Maman, I can't leave you and Bubbe—"

"You can and you will," Mme. Einhorn insisted, her eyes

hard. She looked at Nicole. "I have no right to ask this of you, but will you help me get Claire out of this place? Your father is going to come, eventually. But no one is going to rescue my Claire."

Nicole wanted to refuse. Her father could come for her at any moment, though she was beginning to worry that he did not know where she was. What if he came while she was helping Claire? The French police were behaving like Nazi swine. Who knew what they might do? Why should she risk her freedom, her life, to try to save Claire?

But then, as if some other part of her was in control, Nicole found herself nodding. Yes, she would help.

"Thank you," Mme. Einhorn said, her lips trembling. "Thank you so much." She wasted no time after that, helping Claire change into clothes that had no star, brushing and rebraiding her daughter's hair, and hiding a little money in Claire's socks.

Then they waited. Finally, Nicole could no longer defeat her own body. She barely made it to a wall before tearing her panties aside and squatting like all the others. It had come to this.

As she made her way back to the Einhorns, she heard Mme. Einhorn calling frantically for her. "Nicole, hurry, it's time!" Indeed, the guards were changing their shift.

"Maman," Claire whimpered, clutching at her mother.

"Let go of me," Mme. Einhorn ordered, her voice steely. "Turn around. When you see a big commotion, run."

"Maman—"

"You will run."

Most of the prior shift had gone and only part of the new shift of cops had arrived. Some were holding their noses. But others, judging by their grins and their laughter, were making jokes about the Jews.

"Let's go," Mme. Einhorn decided. She led her daughter over to the new guards as Nicole and Bubbe Einhorn followed. "When do we get water for the children?" she demanded.

"We don't know," a tall cop said.

"We must have water. The children will die of thirst."

Nicole leaned toward Claire and quickly squeezed her hand. Then, she turned to the same cop Mme. Einhorn had confronted. "There is a baby over there, dying," Nicole said, trying to keep her voice from quavering. "He must have water!"

Bubbe Einhorn started babbling in Polish and waving her arms dramatically as Nicole and Mme. Einhorn shouted, "Water for the children, water for the children!"

"Sit down, stop this at once," another policeman ordered.

But Mme. Einhorn and Nicole wouldn't stop. "Water for the children! Water for the children!"

"I am warning you, sit down!" he thundered, his face mottled red with fury.

"Water for the children!" Nicole repeated. The first cop put his hand conspicuously on the butt of his pistol. Nicole froze. She wanted to continue the chant, but no sound came out. She tried again. Nothing. But then, from behind her—

"Water for the children!"

She whirled. It was the pretty girl with the golden hair. "Water for the children!" she repeated, as other women, first in twos and threes, then by dozens, ran to the front gates. Fifty, then more than fifty, many carrying babies, were chanting in the policemen's faces.

"Water for the children! Water for the children!"

From the corner of her eye, Nicole saw Bubbe Einhorn urge Claire forward as the police retreated. Mme. Einhorn raised her voice. "Jewish sisters!" she cried, pointing beyond the gate to a building across the street. "There is a grocery. Let us get water for the children!"

"Halt!" the police yelled, but the women moved as one, pushing into them. In the confusion, Nicole saw Claire's red hair flash by. Then Claire was out the gate.

More cops charged over. They swung truncheons at the crowd. Then a volley of gunfire rang out. Their guns were pointed in the air, but still, the frightening reverberations, and the knowledge that the next volley might be aimed lower, was enough to convince the women that their quest was futile.

The demonstration broke up as quickly as it had begun. Yet Nicole felt strangely happy. No matter what happened now, Claire had escaped. One redheaded Jewish girl had beaten them. As she went back to the stands, Nicole looked for the girl with the golden hair. She wanted to thank her for helping Claire. But she didn't see her anywhere.

sixteen

16 July 1942

It is eight o'clock at night. I never imagined anything on earth could be as bad as this. I saw a woman slash her wrists with broken glass. I watched a father, ranting about how he would not allow his young son to live in such a hell, attempt to strangle his own child. Thank God some people pulled the man off the boy.

Bubbe Einhorn is sick. I think it is the cabbage soup they fed us—one cupful per person. I didn't eat it. Mme. Einhorn is different since Claire escaped. She sits and stares at nothing. She said, "I am no longer a mother. How can I be a mother without a child?"

I try not to betray how frightened I am. Why hasn't Papa come? What if something terrible has happened to him? How do I know that the police have not arrested—

"Nicole!" Mme. Einhorn was shaking her. Nicole looked up from her journal. "Your name was just announced."

"Are you sure?"

"Yes, they said—wait, it's coming on again."

"Attention, attention," a tinny voice announced on the public address system. "Mlle. Nicole Bernhardt is to report to the control area at section one hundred at once. Mlle. Nicole Bernhardt to section one hundred at once."

"My father!" Nicole's heart swelled with hope, her fatigue instantly vanished. Mme. Einhorn tried to smile. Nicole embraced her, then hesitated. Claire's mother had been wonderful to her. "I can't just leave you and Bubbe Einhorn here. She is so sick."

"Nicole, you must go," Mme. Einhorn insisted.

"But—"

"Go."

Nicole kissed Bubbe Einhorn's wrinkled cheek. "I'll tell them to come help. If it's my father, we'll be back. I promise." She grabbed her book bag and her journal, took one last look at Mme. and Bubbe Einhorn, then dodged through the crowd toward section 100.

There, like some dream, stood her father. He looked strong and clean, but his face was a mask of sorrow. He held out his arms to her. She hesitated. "I'm so disgusting, Papa," she whispered.

He enveloped her in his arms. "Oh, my beautiful child," he crooned. "You could never be disgusting. I'm so sorry. I couldn't get in sooner. They wouldn't let anyone in." Nicole realized he was weeping.

"It's all right, Papa. It's not your fault."

A French cop approached them. "Daughter of Dr. Jean Bernhardt, may I see your identity card, please?" Nicole handed it to him. "I apologize, mademoiselle, for your inconvenience. We are only detaining foreigners who do not belong in France and undermine our nation." He bowed slightly to her father. "Docteur Bernhardt, I apologize again. Of course, you are both free to leave."

Nicole turned to her father. "Papa, Bubbe Einhorn is very sick. I promised that you'd help her."

"Of course. They have finally let in a few doctors, but not nearly enough. We must stay and help."

"Not too long, Papa. Please, it's so disgusting here. I can't stand it."

Her father took her by the shoulders. "Yes, you can."

She said nothing. But all through the night, she helped her father tend to the sick, beginning with the Einhorns. Dr. Bernhardt gave Bubbe Einhorn medicine to stop her cramps. "I will do everything in my power to get you both released," he promised.

"There is nothing you can do," Mme. Einhorn replied. "There is nothing anyone can do."

"If anyone can help, it is my father." Nicole hugged Claire's mother. "Do not lose hope. Please."

From the Einhorns they moved on to a woman in labor.

On the floor of the Vel, surrounded by a cordon of women, Nicole helped her father deliver the baby—a perfect little girl who gave a lusty cry. Even in that horrid place, it was an awesome moment.

But Nicole had no time to think about the baby, because the next patient was in the midst of a terrible asthma attack. As hard as Dr. Bernhardt tried, he could not save the man, who choked to death in his arms. Her father quickly said Kaddish, the Jewish prayer for the dead. Nicole wept softly. They moved on to treat more of the living.

It felt to Nicole as if a lifetime had passed when she and her father finally stepped out onto the rue Nelaton. It was just before dawn. 17 July 1942. A new day.

Amazing. The streets were peaceful, empty. How could it be? People must have heard the news, or seen the buses heading to the Vel. In the past, Nicole knew, Parisians had risen up in armed fury over much less than this atrocity. But the city slept, as if the 8,000 Jews in the Vel did not exist.

In silence, they walked home, crossing the Seine, climbing the stone staircase that Nicole had descended twenty-four hours earlier. She felt like an animal who had shed one skin and donned another, tougher one. All doubt was gone. The man holding her hand was her father and had always been her father. She was and always had been Nicole Bernhardt, born in 1927, who lived in Paris, France. A Jew.

Once, she had imagined that she lived in the future, in America. But like a wisp of smoke that rises from dying embers and disappears on a spring wind, it was gone forever.

s e v e n t e e n

18 October 1942

I *have wonderful news. C is alive! In today's post
came a card from her. It was unsigned but it is obvious that it is C and that she is living with a Catholic
family. I am not going to write her name in case my
journal falls into the wrong hands, but here is what
the postcard said:*

Life is fine in Oradour-sur-Glane. I am planning my
wedding to a very plain but intelligent boy. Should we
serve smoked salmon or roast chicken? I am studying
my catechism every day.

*It made me feel so happy to hear from her. She did
not write about her father. Perhaps she will send
another card soon.*

*It still eats away at me that Papa was not able to
help Mme. and Bubbe E. I remember when I
believed he could do anything. I wonder where that*

innocent—or should I say, stupid—girl went? He made many inquiries with the authorities but he was not able to get them released from either the Vel or from Drancy.

It is amazing to me how normal much of life is. We hear that the movie houses, theaters, and cabarets are full every night, French publishing houses bring out new books by famous writers; there are posters everywhere advertising it all. Many people go to see German entertainers, which I find deplorable. Even if Jews were permitted to go, I would never attend. The slang term "waiter" is used for people who just go about their daily business and wait *for the Occupation to end. It seems like it is going to be a very long wait.*

I had the most terrible dream last night where Jacques was in love with Suzanne. But he loves me. He does. He comes over almost every day. We go to my room and kiss with the door closed. Liz-Bette always hovers outside, and if she doesn't hear us talking for five minutes she runs and tells Maman. Then Maman finds a pretext to disturb us. I am certain she thinks that we are too young to spend that much time together behind closed doors, but it is not as if life were normal. There is a war on!

Nicole huddled in her winter coat on the living room window seat, looking down on the rainy, blustery November morning. A few miserable-looking pedestrians fought the elements. Still, her parents allowed her to go outside so infrequently that Nicole would have given anything to feel the rain pelting her.

She checked her watch as the familiar anxious feeling in the pit of her stomach grew. Jacques had promised to come by before he went to school. He was already ten minutes late. A few more minutes and it meant he wouldn't come at all. Though he swore he loved her as much as ever, Nicole was feeling increasingly insecure about their relationship—the less freedom she had, the more insecure she became.

The latest blow was that her father had announced that she and Liz-Bette could no longer go to school because of the danger of a tuberculosis outbreak. It was infuriating. She loved walking to and from school with Jacques, their arms linked. She even loved how some people would stare at them—the handsome blond boy and the Jewish girl with the yellow star. School had been one of the few places the Nazis still allowed Jews to go. Now, her parents—not the Germans—had taken that away from her. How could they?

As she stared down at the street, Liz-Bette began to play the violin in her bedroom, the Hatikva theme from Smetana's "The Moldau." Nicole winced at the usual assortment of incorrect notes. "Can you please for once play another song?" Nicole called.

Liz-Bette came into the living room, violin under her arm. "It's the only piece I know by heart. My teacher won't teach me anymore because I'm Jewish. Do you find that fair? Because I don't."

Nicole didn't answer. She looked down the street for Jacques again. It was empty.

"Nicole?"

"What?"

"Do you ever . . . do you ever wish you weren't Jewish?"

Nicole finally turned to regard her sister, sitting on the couch. She looked tiny, in two oversized sweaters. "Why are you asking?"

"It would be very terrible, I know it would." Liz-Bette bit nervously at her lower lip. "I am a terrible person."

Nicole went to sit beside her. "Did something happen?"

"Do you remember Liliane Stryker? She moved here from Belgium. She was the prettiest girl in my form. I was jealous because I thought I was only second prettiest. I thought maybe we were both safe because we have blue eyes and blond hair. But the police came right into our class at school and took her away on a big bus, and we're never going to see her again. Ever since then, I have been wishing I was a Catholic girl so that no one will take me away on a big bus."

"No one is going to take you away, Liz-Bette."

"How do you know?"

"Well, for one thing, we are French and they are deporting very few French Jews. You remember what happened with me at the Vel. And for another, Papa has an Ausweis."

Liz-Bette looked thoughtful. "That's true. I like being Jewish, Nicole. I just don't like being scared. You won't tell Papa?"

"I won't," Nicole promised.

The front door opened, and Dr. Bernhardt stepped into the apartment. He had been upstairs writing in his study. "Two tragic faces," he commented. "Liz-Bette, don't you have schoolwork to do?"

"Yes, Papa," Liz-Bette said obediently. "Maman is a much harder teacher at home than any of my real teachers were at school." She trudged off to her room. Nicole went back to the window.

No sign of Jacques. It meant she wouldn't see him until after school at the earliest. Idly, she swiped her index finger along the window glass, writing his name in the condensation that had begun to form.

"You were expecting Jacques, little one?" Dr. Bernhardt asked.

Nicole was afraid that if she answered, she would cry.

And she didn't want to cry. So she changed the subject. "Please say you'll let us go back to school soon, Papa."

"Perhaps you see the humor in that remark. You were never too keen on going to school before."

Nicole sighed and turned back to the window. It was raining harder than ever.

"Nicole?"

"Yes, Papa?"

"I understand how difficult this is for you."

Did he really? How could he? No one had taken away every bit of his freedom when he was young.

"Yes, Papa."

He considered her for a moment. "I am on my way to visit patients at one of the UGIF old age homes. Would you like to come with me?"

"I don't understand. If you won't allow me to go to school because you are concerned about a tuberculosis epidemic—"

"That is only a partial truth," her father admitted. He came to her. "Ever since the Vel d'Hiv roundup, your mother has been terrified of letting you and Liz-Bette out of her sight. I persuaded her to let you girls return to school this fall. But the incident with the Stryker girl was too much even for me. We feel safer with you here. I am sure that your mother will feel relatively safe to have you out with your papa. Will you come with me?"

Nicole readily agreed. She'd go anywhere if it meant getting out of the apartment. She hurried to get her identity card before her father could change his mind.

∽

Dr. Bernhardt took the pulse of an old woman who had broken her hip. She reminded Nicole of Bubbe Einhorn, with a long white braid. "Your pulse is strong and your hip is mending well, Madame Nadler," her father pronounced. "I think you can begin to use a walker in the hallways."

She nodded. "Thank you, Docteur Bernhardt. I do not know what I would do without this place. And you."

Nicole's father pulled a chair up to Mme. Nadler's bedside. He asked after her family, as he had done all morning long with each elderly person he had examined. Most were immigrants who spoke poor French, but her father had listened patiently as they poured their hearts out to him. Nicole didn't see how he could bear it.

"They shot my grandson Mounie, Docteur Bernhardt."

"I am so sorry."

"He edited *The Yellow Star*. A so-called friend betrayed him."

Nicole shuddered. She knew that *The Yellow Star* was an underground Yiddish newspaper. Her father spoke with Mme. Nadler a little longer, then kissed her on each cheek.

Nicole said a polite good-bye and followed her father into the hall. "Will Mme. Nadler be able to go home soon?"

"Considering what has happened to her grandson, I feel certain that her medical condition will not permit her to leave here." Dr. Bernhardt looked at Nicole sharply. "Do you understand?"

"Do you mean she's safer here, Papa? Can't the Boche—"

A hearty voice called from down the hallway. "Good morning, Docteur Bernhardt!" Coming toward them was a young man so handsome that he took Nicole's breath away—tall and muscular, with electric blue eyes, glossy chestnut hair, and a cleft in his chin just like Clark Gable's. He wore a Gestapo uniform.

Nicole looked quickly at her father. His face betrayed nothing. "Good morning, Inspector Gruber," Dr. Bernhardt said politely.

The young Nazi's eyes fell on Nicole. "And who is this lovely young lady?"

"My daughter," her father said.

"But you must make us a proper introduction," the young man insisted, in excellent French. "It is not every day that I come upon a sight so lovely in a home for old Jews."

Dr. Bernhardt hesitated, then said, "Inspector Gruber, may I present my daughter, Mlle. Nicole Bernhardt."

"Enchanted." The Gestapo officer brought Nicole's hand to his lips. Only fear kept her from snatching it back and wiping it off on her sweater.

"I am the Gestapo liaison to this establishment," Inspector Gruber explained pleasantly. "But we needn't be so formal. After all, I am not so much older than you, mademoiselle, I suspect. Your age is?"

"Fifteen."

"Charming. What do you do for enjoyment, Mademoiselle Bernhardt?"

Her father took her arm. "If you will excuse us, Inspector Gruber, I still have patients to see."

"Just another moment, if you please. Your lovely daughter has not had the opportunity to answer my question. Mademoiselle?"

"I . . . see my friends."

The inspector nodded earnestly. "Friends and family are the most important things. Especially during such trying times. Your father, the famous Dr. Bernhardt, also values his wonderful family and friends. So many people love and respect him so very much. I am sure you are very proud of him."

"Yes."

"His contributions to the UGIF are valuable. That is why he has been granted an Ausweis. It would be a terrible loss if he were to disappear. We should be forced to seek out his family and friends—perhaps also *your* friends—in an effort to locate him. That is how dearly he would be missed."

Dr. Bernhardt took Nicole's arm again. "We really must be going, Inspector Gruber. I must finish my rounds."

"Yes, of course." The German bowed to Dr. Bernhardt and then to Nicole. "It was a pleasure to meet you, Mademoiselle Bernhardt. I hope to see you again soon. By the way, it would be unfortunate should you decide to ignore what I said. You would find your way far more difficult. I bid you both a good day."

As Nicole's father steered her away, the Gestapo officer called out once more. "Mademoiselle?"

Nicole stopped. Inspector Gruber walked over, took something from his jacket pocket, and pressed it into her hand. It was a bar of real chocolate, something she hadn't seen in a very long time. "For your little sister," he told her. "I understand that she is quite a beauty."

Her father led her down the hallway. When they rounded the corner, Nicole dropped the precious chocolate into a trash bin as if it had been poisoned.

nineteen

NOTES FROM GIRL X

21 November 1942

To the people of Paris,
When my father told me that I could no longer attend school, I felt helpless. Trapped. But then, I got an idea. I asked my friend M if she would help. She agreed, because she is courageous.

Dear reader, you hold in your hands an entry from the diary of Girl X, an ordinary adolescent girl in the City of Light. She is French. She believes in "liberty, equality, and fraternity." She is Jewish. She despises the Boche and those French traitors who help them. During the day, she recopies journal entries onto sheets of paper like this—three, four, five copies—however many she can accomplish. Her friend M visits her after school, takes the copies of Girl X's journal, and secretly leaves them places for you to find. On a park bench. At the Trocadéro metro station. In the Tuileries. On a movie seat. Where did you find this, dear reader?

I am Girl X, now being taught at home by my mother. Regular subjects in the morning, Torah study in the afternoon. We light Shabbos candles on Friday night. Maman puts them out after only a few minutes so that we can conserve them. Then Papa makes a kiddush with whatever there is to drink, puts his hands on my head and then on my sister's, and blesses us. Yivarechecha Adonai viyismerecha. *For that instant, the world feels perfectly safe to me again.*

But it is not safe, dear reader. This we know. The Allies have invaded North Africa, and the Boche have occupied our entire country to guard the southern coast. When will the invasion of Europe come? When?

twenty

NOTES FROM GIRL X

3 December 1942

To *the people of Paris,*

Yesterday I awoke at five o'clock because I knew that J would visit before school. J is the boy I love. He brought me news and in some ways I wish he had not. His older brother has fallen in love with an actress. She acts in plays that are approved by the Nazis. J said she claims to be above politics. I told him it is wrong for her to perform on stage when there are Boche swine in the audience. We had an argument and I feel terrible.

Every day my life is the same. Inside I am changing but I am allowed no new experiences, no way to express these changes. It makes me want to scream. I read books to lift me out of this dreary world and into another where I am not hungry all the time. There is still no food. Thank God for what J and M bring us. We eat beans almost every day.

The Nazis are attacking Russia near Stalingrad. My father says they should have paid more attention to French history, because Napoleon met his greatest defeat in Russia. In my opinion, even if the Germans freeze to death in Russia, the eastern front is still very far from France.

Dear reader, I implore you, do not remain indifferent to the terrible things that the Boche and their traitor friends are doing. Even elderly Jews from a UGIF home have been sent to Drancy. What are they going to do with old people? They cannot work! If you are free to read this, you are free to help. Why do you not all write letters to the Pope? Some of you are certainly happy writing letters to the Gestapo, denouncing Jews.

twenty-one

23 February 1943

Nicole stood on a chair and peered over her shoulder at Mimi, who drew a line with an eyebrow pencil up the back of Nicole's leg.

"It's not supposed to snake around like that," Nicole protested.

"Well, hold still, and it won't."

"Does it look like a stocking seam?"

Liz-Bette put down the book she was reading and came over to pass judgment. "No," she pronounced. "It looks like someone drew a line up your leg."

"Who are you, the new style editor of *For Her* magazine?" Nicole teased, as she stepped down from the chair.

"I would be a very good editor. And then I could have real stockings." Liz-Bette climbed onto the chair.

"After the war," Nicole sighed.

"After the war, after the war, everything is after the war," Liz-Bette complained. "But the war just goes on and on. Do my legs, Mimi." She posed one palm up, the other on her hip, like a runway model.

"A line on your leg will look just as ridiculous on you as on me," Nicole pointed out.

"I don't care." Liz-Bette lifted her three layers of skirts, worn to ward off the cold.

"Your wish is my command, mademoiselle." Mimi dropped to a knee and began to draw up the back of Liz-Bette's right leg.

Liz-Bette struck another pose. "This is what American girls do, you know. I wish I were American. I could meet Clark Gable and he would fall madly in love with me."

"His wife just died, Liz-Bette," Mimi said.

"And you're eleven," Nicole added.

Liz-Bette shrugged. "So? I'm a broad-minded woman."

"Ugh, that's what Monique always says," Mimi groaned, as she started to work on Liz-Bette's left leg. "Nicole, did Jacques tell you that she and André are now officially engaged? He's bringing her over tonight to celebrate—her director at the City Theatre gave her a ten-year-old bottle of calvados."

A hard lump of resentment welled up in Nicole's throat. The party for André and Monique's engagement would be yet another event that she would have to miss because of the Jewish curfew. "It sounds like fun," she admitted.

"It won't be," Mimi assured her. "Monique is loathsome. I can assure you, you won't see her getting skinny, because she wines and dines with the enemy. And her best friend, Simone, is pregnant by one of the Boche."

Nicole made a face of disgust. "Now, that is loathsome."

"How can André be with her?" Liz-Bette asked.

Mimi rolled her eyes. "He claims to love her for her pure artistic spirit. Personally, I think it's because she looks like Hedy Lamarr."

Liz-Bette sniffed. "That is very shallow."

"But Jacques says André is a hero," Nicole protested.

"My twin is supremely juvenile. I don't know whom he worships more, André or your father."

Nicole used her handkerchief to rub out the line on the back of her leg. "It's more than that. Jacques said that last week André was ordered to pick up some Polish Jews. He went to their apartment and told them he was coming back for them in fifteen minutes, so that they'd have time to get away. And they did."

"That's heroic," Liz-Bette decreed.

Mimi shrugged. "Perhaps. But it would be more heroic if he quit the police and refused to work with the wretched Hun pigs altogether."

"He'd just be sent to Germany to work for the wretched Hun pigs anyway," Nicole pointed out.

Of all the edicts the Nazis had implemented in France, none were as hated by most French people as the STO, the Service du Travail Obligatoire. Under it, the Nazis were now drafting French young men to work on German soil in place of soldiers who were fighting the Allies.

Mimi recapped the eyebrow pencil. "Some things are worth fighting for, Nicole."

Liz-Bette nervously twisted the end of one blond braid.

"What if we got taken away on a big bus before André could warn us?"

Mimi and Nicole traded looks. "That will never happen to a magnificent French beauty like you, Liz-Bette," Mimi finally said. "There. All done. You are the epitome of Parisian chic."

Liz-Bette jumped down and paraded around the room like a runway model while Mimi and Nicole oohed and aahed dramatically. That made Liz-Bette giggle, which made Nicole and Mimi laugh, too. Mme. Bernhardt ran into the living room.

"What is that noise?" she demanded. Exclamation points of anxiety were etched between her eyes.

"Nothing, Maman," Nicole assured her. "We were just laughing."

"Nicole, call me the instant your father—"

The front door opened and Dr. Bernhardt wearily entered the flat. "Papa!" Liz-Bette ran to hug him.

He kissed the top of her head. "Hello, little one." He hung up his hat but kept his coat on against the cold.

"Mimi, I'm afraid I must ask you to leave," Mme. Bernhardt said. "We have family business to take care of."

"But Mimi is practically a member of the family," Liz-Bette protested. "In fact, why don't we exchange her for Nicole?"

"I am in no mood for your foolishness, young lady," Mme. Bernhardt snapped. "Please forgive my rudeness, Mimi."

"It's all right. I have to leave anyway." Mimi put on her beret, embraced Nicole, and slipped out the front door.

As soon as she was gone, Mme. Bernhardt turned to her daughters. "Girls, sit down." Her tone was so abrupt that Nicole was taken aback.

"Renée?" Dr. Bernhardt asked.

"Sit!"

Nicole and Liz-Bette took seats on the couch. Mme. Bernhardt locked eyes with her husband. "It is about your so-called upstairs office."

He paled. "Let the children go to their rooms."

"There is no time for them to be children now, you have seen to that." She pulled something from her apron and held out her hand. Nicole stretched to see what she had. Bullets. Her mother was holding bullets. Mme. Bernhardt forced them into her husband's hand. "You use bullets now for medical writing?" She extracted something else from her pocket—it looked to Nicole like a clock, except that there were wires extending from it. "And this? A timer for a bomb?"

"Yes," Dr. Bernhardt said.

"Have you lost your mind?" Mme. Bernhardt smashed the timer to the floor, where it shattered into a million pieces.

"I didn't want you to worry, Renée."

Mme. Bernhardt laughed bitterly. "Why should I worry? Just because you are making bombs over the heads of our children?"

"Renée, please—"

"Just because you have taken the one place, the only

place that these children can feel safe, and you have turned it into a bomb factory?"

"Perhaps I should have told you sooner—"

"Perhaps?"

"Yes. You are right," Dr. Bernhardt agreed. "Every single day I planned to tell you. But I kept putting it off." He removed his glasses, put them in his pocket, then looked at his wife again. "I work in the Resistance, Renée. With Solidarity."

Nicole gasped as all the color drained from her mother's face. "Jean, Solidarity? They are Reds. Communists!"

"Not all of them. I am not. It's very important work—"

"Important enough to risk your children's lives?"

"I have to do this, Renée—"

"Do you? You foolish man!" Nicole's stomach lurched. She had never, ever heard her mother speak this way to their father. "A scrawny band of underfed Jews and Communists trying to defeat Hitler? He crushed the entire French army in five weeks, Jean. Five weeks!"

"I cannot lie down and die. I won't."

"So you make bombs?" Mme. Bernhardt's tone was scathing. "And what happens when your bombs go off and kill some Nazis, eh? There are reprisals. You see the posters. For every Nazi you kill, they will shoot one hundred Jews."

"They will shoot one hundred Jews anyway, Renée. And one hundred more, and one hundred more, until there are no more Jews—"

"Foreign Jews! They are taking only foreign Jews."

Dr. Bernhardt looked at his wife with more sadness than anger. "You do not mean this, Renée."

She set her chin defiantly. "I do mean it. We are French. They will not take French Jews who do not bother them."

"Renée, listen to me—"

"No. I will not listen. Do you realize how foolish you are? By night you shoot Nazis. By day you are a doctor for a Jewish hospital where the Nazis find Jews to shoot in reprisal for who *you* shot the night before." Mme. Bernhardt threw her hands in the air. "Do you not see the lunacy of this?"

Nicole watched her father's shoulders sag. For a long moment, he didn't speak. Then, finally, he said, "In a war, many things happen which do not make perfect sense, Renée. Perhaps I am foolish. But I must do it. Please try to understand—"

"No. What I care about is my family," she declared. "And surviving. Surviving!"

"It's going to get worse, Renée. We can't just—"

"We can," she insisted. "My family has lived in Paris for four generations. My father was wounded at Verdun in '17. You are a famous doctor. We are French. And if we are careful, we can survive until the Allies come."

Nicole had never seen her father look as sad as he did at that moment, when he tenderly touched her mother's cheek. "My darling wife. I wish it were so simple. But it is not." He turned to his daughters. "You must listen carefully to what I am about to say. We may have to go into hiding."

Liz-Bette shook her head violently, as if she could will it not to be true. Something tickled the edge of Nicole's mind. What was it? Something that someone had said about her father. But who? And where? Yes! She had it. It was that Gestapo inspector, the one she'd met at the UGIF home. He had said it would be terrible idea if Dr. Bernhardt were to disappear. And now—

"If we must go into hiding, we must make everyone believe we have been deported," her father continued.

Nicole was startled. "Even Jacques and Mimi?"

Her father hesitated. "Invite Jacques to my office at the hospital. They may be the ones to help us, if they are willing. But they must never know that I am with Solidarity. No one must know. Do you understand, Liz-Bette?"

Liz-Bette nodded, her lower lip trembling. Nicole was still desperately trying to reconstruct the conversation at the UGIF home. Hadn't the inspector said something about their friends, some kind of threat? Oh, God. Did the lousy Hun already suspect that her father might be in the underground? Was he having their flat watched even now? If they were to disappear, what might he do to Jacques and Mimi?

"All of you, listen to me," her mother commanded. "Stop this nonsense. We are not hiding like rats in a sewer. It is out of the question."

Dr. Bernhardt met her gaze. "We will do what we have to do. Now, if my unit gets word to me that I have been denounced, or if I am taken—"

"This is insane, Jean," Mme. Bernhardt cried. "For God's sake, all you have to do is stop!"

"That I cannot do."

"Even if it means your life?"

Nicole felt as if she could choke on the silence, waiting for her father's answer. He said nothing, which was the most painful answer of all.

"I don't want to live without you," her mother told him.

Her father—or someone who looked like her father— pointed to the front door. "If someone should come and say this code word—Nightbird—the code word is Nightbird. Repeat it." He looked sharply at his daughters.

"Nightbird," Nicole and Liz-Bette repeated.

"If that should happen, you must leave here instantly. You will walk to seventeen, rue Saint André des Arts in the sixth district, near the Saint-Michel metro—"

"No, Papa!" Liz-Bette ran to him.

He held her away from him roughly, so he could see her face. "Repeat the address for me."

"You're scaring me, Papa."

"Repeat the address. Now!"

Nicole joined Liz-Bette and linked arms with her sister. "It's all right, Liz-Bette. Say the address with me. Seventeen—"

"Rue Saint André des Arts," Liz-Bette joined in softly.

"You will see a man named Luçon," Dr. Bernhardt instructed. "Say his name."

"Luçon."

Dr. Bernhardt turned to his wife. She was at the window, gazing into the Paris night. "Please, Renée," he said quietly. "I am begging you. Seventeen . . . seventeen . . ."

Nicole held her breath. Finally, her mother's lips moved, in the softest whisper. "Seventeen, rue Saint André des Arts."

Relief flooded her father's face. "Luçon."

"Luçon."

"He will arrange for your hiding. If I can, I will join you there. You children must memorize the address, in case you are separated from your mother. You will leave immediately. Wear as many layers of clothes as you can. Do not wear the star. Do not carry anything. Make sure you are not followed. Do not tell anyone where you are going—"

Liz-Bette looked up at the stranger who now inhabited her father's body. "I don't want to leave you, Papa."

He looked down at her. And finally, it was her beloved father who answered. "I don't want to leave you, either, little one."

Mme. Bernhardt came to her husband. "If we live through this, Jean, I will be mad at you for the rest of our lives."

Dr. Bernhardt smiled sadly. "*When* we live through this, Renée, I won't blame you." With one arm wrapped around Liz-Bette, he held the other out to his wife. She embraced him. Nicole put her arms around all of them.

There was nothing more to say.

NOTES FROM GIRL X

20 April 1943

To *the people of Paris,*

Happy birthday to me. This is quite a boring way for Girl X to spend her sixteenth birthday, don't you think? For it is the exact same way she spent the day before and the day before that and the day before that. At least J and M have promised to bring birthday presents when they come over later. In any case, here is how one Jewish girl whose parents will no longer send her to school uses her time:

9:00 A.M. Wake up after sleeping as long as possible. The warmest place in our apartment is my bed, and when I am sleeping I can dream of food.

9:20 A.M. Breakfast. Today, Viandox, that horrid substitute for coffee. Dried bread from yesterday.

10:00 A.M.–1:00 P.M. Studies with Maman. History, English, mathematics, literature, science, and sociology. I dread mathematics. Maman is a mathe-

matics wizard and loves to torture me. What use could I possibly ever have for all these equations? English is enjoyable because Maman never learned it so we are all studying together. LB picks it up fastest. The only good thing about not going to school is that I do not have to study German.

1:00 P.M.–1:30 P.M. Midday meal. Today: rutabaga. Yesterday: rutabaga. The day before yesterday: surprise! Rutabaga and vermicelli.

1:30 P.M.–2:45 P.M. Jewish studies.

2:45 P.M.–4:00 P.M. Maman shops with our ration cards. Usually this is when I write these notes. Sometimes LB and I play chess. I like the game very much. You use your wits to play at war, but no one gets deported or killed.

4:00 P.M.–5:00 P.M. J and M come to visit. Bliss! Especially when M leaves so J and I can be alone. The minutes are crawling by right now as I wait for him. Lately I've been longing for more than just kisses. Our love is eternal, so how can it be wrong for us to allow a physical expression of it? Why must it be "You can touch this part of my body, but that part is forbidden"? Who makes such ridiculous rules? Maman is so old-fashioned about these things. Here is what she told me about why I should remain a virgin: "If there are two identical sweaters in a shop window, and one is perfect and untouched, but the other is wrinkly and used, which sweater would you buy?"

LB was eavesdropping and she blurted out, "N is not a sweater!" I loved her very much at that moment.

5:00 P.M.–7:00 P.M. Two hours spent missing J and waiting for Papa to come home. Sometimes he does, sometimes he does not. I do not want to say more.

7:00 P.M.–8:00 P.M. Dinner. Tonight will be a birthday feast! Roast potatoes, carrots, and some dandelion greens that Maman was able to secure on the black market.

8:00 P.M. Forbidden radio, volume very low, if the electricity is operating, if the Boche are not jamming the BBC, and if our idiot concierge is not poking around our building looking for someone to denounce. In case you do not have a radio, the BBC reported that the Russians have retaken quite a bit of territory, and that American planes bombed Bremen. Sixteen B-17s were lost.

8:30 P.M. Bed. I am never sleepy but the warmth of my bed calls to me so I bring a book or my journal and—

Hold on. I'll be back. J and M are here!

Hello, I'm back. I had such a wonderful time. M brought me a record of the Andrews Sisters, very jazzy. J brought me a new journal he found on the black market. It is so beautiful, with a thick leather cover and paper so creamy that you can practically taste it. Do you see why I love J so? If I close my eyes, I can still feel his lips on mine, my body pressed to his. Tonight I felt so passionately in love with him that I thought I would die with desire. He whispered in my ear that he wanted to make love to me. It is the first time he said the words.

Love is freedom. It is something the Boche can never take from me.

twenty-three

NOTES FROM GIRL X

10 September 1943

To the people of Paris,
   Dear reader, if you are reading this and are not a collabo idiot, please put this under the door of someone who is. Thank you.

Hello, Collabo Idiot! I am a Jewish girl forbidden now by my parents to leave our home, but still you cannot silence my voice. I hear there are wanted posters plastered everywhere, seeking the culprit who threw a grenade into the headquarters of your collabo friend Jacques Doriot's PPF party and wounded fifteen people. They have already shot many innocents in reprisal and say they will randomly kill more each day until the culprit is apprehended. Does that fill you with joy? I also hear there is V-for-victory graffiti everywhere, even on the wanted posters. Here is one more for good measure!

Hear me, Collabo Idiot. Your Boche masters have lost their ally Italy. The Allied invasion of Europe will come. You will not win. Yes, you denounce Jews in exchange for extra rations. Yes, you eat while we starve. Yes, you laugh in the sun while we cower in the shadows. But not forever. The righteous shall triumph. Long live France!

twenty-four

31 December 1943

"Maman?" Nicole asked. "Are you awake? I brought you some leek soup." She set the soup on the night table by her parents' bed. Other than a few detestable rutabaga, those leeks were the last food left in the flat, and they had no more ration coupons. Tomorrow was New Year's; that meant the shops would be closed. Unless her father brought home food from the hospital—an unlikely possibility—they would be living on air for the next thirty-six hours.

At least the Rothschild Hospital was still permitted to function, Nicole thought. But that was only so that sick and injured Jews wouldn't have to be brought to other hospitals.

"Maman?" Nicole whispered again. Her mother's eyes barely opened. She, who never got sick, had been ill for days. Dr. Bernhardt had assured them it was influenza and not tuberculosis. But so far as Nicole could tell, her mother didn't seem to be improving.

"I made soup for you. I'll fix the pillows so you can sit up and eat," Nicole offered.

"I am not hungry."

"But you must eat. Papa says—"

"Yes, I am well aware of what Papa says. You girls quote him so much you would think he was Maimonides."

Nicole grinned. That remark had sounded like Maman's normal self. "Maimonides was also a doctor, you know. Papa and I have been studying *The Guide for the Perplexed*."

"What perplexes me is why I am not improving." Mme. Bernhardt's eyelids began to droop. "Is there food for you and your sister?"

"We're fine. Rest now."

Within moments, her mother was snoring. Nicole tucked the covers under her chin, then carried the soup back to the kitchen, where Liz-Bette sat at the table studying a chess problem. When she saw the full soup bowl, she perked up immediately. "May I have it?"

Nicole put the soup in front of her. "You could show some concern that Maman didn't eat."

"I am concerned. I am also hungry."

Worry gnawed at Nicole as she watched her sister greedily shovel soup into her mouth. Liz-Bette had grown so thin. But everyone in Paris was hungry. The only people who weren't ran food shops or were cooperating with the Nazis. There were pictures in the newspapers all the time of the actress Danielle Darrieux. She looked healthy, indeed.

Liz-Bette slurped up the last of the soup and stared forlornly into the empty bowl. "We need more food."

"That is called stating the obvious, Liz-Bette. Shall we ask the ghost of Harry Houdini to conjure some up for us?"

Liz-Bette laughed, but it faded quickly. Nicole had to figure out a way to get more food—real food, with protein. Her mother needed it to get well. Even when her father brought home food from the hospital it was always vegetables, not the protein that her mother needed. And who was to say he was coming home tonight, in any case? There were times they did not see him for three days at a time, about which he would say nothing.

Though her parents had forbidden it, there was only one thing to do, Nicole decided. She headed for the living room. Liz-Bette clomped along behind her. Nicole grabbed the two ornate silver candlesticks from atop the grand piano. "What are you doing?" Liz-Bette asked nervously.

"What does it look like I'm doing?" From the coat rack, Nicole took an old coat of her father's, a yellow star sewn to the outside. She reached into the pocket and found a few francs. Perfect, she thought. Money for the metro.

"Nicole, you can't sell Maman's candlesticks on the black market."

"Do you want to eat?"

"Yes. But we aren't supposed to go out."

"We aren't supposed to starve, either." Nicole stuck the heavy candlesticks into an interior coat pocket.

"If you are going, I am going with you," Liz-Bette declared.

"No. You stay here. In case Maman needs you."

"You are not my mother," Liz-Bette said calmly, as she put on one of her mother's jackets. It hung loosely, even with all the sweaters she was wearing.

The sisters stared at each other. The Gestapo and the Permilleux Service had taken to arresting Jews on the flimsiest of pretexts, making no distinction between Jews of French citizenship and refugees. If they were caught . . . Nicole pushed the thought from her mind.

"Come on, then." Nicole grabbed a mesh shopping bag from its hook on the wall. "No, wait." She replaced the mesh bag and took a small valise from the front hall closet, thinking that at least no one could see what was inside a valise.

Silently, they walked downstairs, passing the Einhorns' old flat. A French family lived there now, the Duponts. After the Vel d'Hiv roundup, the government had requisitioned the flat and allocated it to the Duponts, who had taken all the Einhorns' furniture as their own.

Moments later, they were outside in the sunshine. It was chilly, but the air felt wonderful. Liz-Bette tilted her face to the sun. "We have no time for that," Nicole said, though she felt like doing exactly the same thing. "Come on."

They walked briskly to the Trocadéro metro station, paid their fares, and waited for the train to arrive, careful not to make eye contact with anyone. They boarded the last car—the only car in which Jews were allowed to ride—and took it to the Porte de Clignancourt station at the north end of Paris. Near the station was the flea market—well known as a site for black market dealings.

They joined the crowds strolling past the pathetic assortments of goods it was still legal to sell: old cosmetics, paper fans, household goods, costume jewelry, and the like.

"There's no food here," Liz-Bette grumbled.

Nicole eyed a nearby garbage bin. A young woman dangled from the top as she rummaged through it, her panties exposed. "Never," Liz-Bette declared, catching sight of the girl. "I will not dive into garbage. It is disgusting."

"We will see." Nicole took her sister's arm. People eyed their yellow stars—sometimes with sympathy, sometimes with contempt, most often with apathy.

Liz-Bette shrank into Nicole's side. "Maybe we should just go home." Nicole ignored her, trying to come up with a plan. How was she going to find someone willing to trade food for her candlesticks?

From behind her, someone called, "Nicole! Nicole Bernhardt!"

Run! Her instincts commanded, but she fought them. Running would only focus attention on her and her sister. Instead, she calmly turned around.

It wasn't the Gestapo, thank God. It was her former classmate Suzanne Lebeau, whom she hadn't seen since she'd left school. "Oh, how I've missed you!" Suzanne cried, throwing her arms around Nicole. "And you, too, Liz-Bette."

When Suzanne stepped back, Nicole saw that her old friend was as beautiful as ever—sophisticated-looking, in fact. Her hair was held back with stylish twin combs. She wore a lovely red coat, red high heels, and matching lipstick.

She even had on silk stockings. Nicole pulled her father's shabby coat closer around her neck.

"Tell me, how are you doing?" Suzanne asked.

"Fine," Nicole lied.

Suzanne frowned. "No, not *fine*. That was stupid of me. I am so sorry I haven't been to see you but—"

"Mimi told me," Nicole said stiffly. "Your parents will no longer allow you to associate with Jews. We should be going." She reached for Liz-Bette's arm.

"Wait." Suzanne buried her hands farther into her fur muff. "What are you doing here?"

"Jews are still allowed here."

"No, I meant . . ." Suzanne hesitated. "I am here with my mother. Our rich relatives and their friends are coming to dinner tonight. I hate these relatives. But my mother is desperate for crystal goblets, to make a good impression. Do you understand?"

Was she saying her rich relatives were collaborators, their friends Huns? Was she offering to help them? But who knew if her parents weren't collaborators, too? Nicole saw Liz-Bette shake her head imperceptibly, meaning she didn't want Nicole to tell. The whole thing was a risk. But silence was not going to feed them.

"I have my mother's silver candlesticks and I need to barter them for food," Nicole said bluntly.

Suzanne tapped her rouged lips thoughtfully with the tip of one finger. "Ah! I know. Come with me. But take off your coats with the stars on them. Please."

Nicole hesitated now. Was she walking into a trap? But she shrugged off her coat anyway, as did Liz-Bette, and then followed as Suzanne led them through the crowd at a pace that left undernourished Nicole and Liz-Bette breathless.

They halted before an elderly couple with leathery skin. Both wore farmers' coveralls. Before them, on wood pallets, were handmade dolls laid out in neat rows. Suzanne began a whispered exchange with the woman, who whispered back, shaking her head emphatically. The woman's finger stabbed the air at the yellow star peeking out from the coat draped over Nicole's arm.

Suzanne turned to Nicole. "Go to the corner. Wait there."

"But—"

"Just do it."

Feeling helpless, Nicole took Liz-Bette's arm and walked twenty paces toward the corner. "I'm f-f-freezing," Liz-Bette said, teeth chattering. As Nicole gave her sister one of her sweaters, Suzanne brushed past them with the old man.

"Come on," she hissed, over her shoulder. "Before he changes his mind."

Out of the flea market and down a side street they went, struggling to keep up with the old man's brisk pace. "Where are we going?" Liz-Bette asked Nicole.

"I don't know."

"Then we shouldn't go," Liz-Bette insisted, hanging back.

"It's all right," Suzanne assured her. "Just hurry."

The old man led them to a dilapidated building several blocks away. He let himself in, motioning that Suzanne should come with him but Nicole and Liz-Bette should wait on the street. Again, Nicole wondered if they were walking into a trap.

A minute passed. Two. They stamped their feet to try to keep warm. She was about to tell Liz-Bette they should leave when the front door opened and Suzanne appeared. "Come on!"

They walked up a dark stairwell that smelled of rotten cabbage. From someone's phonograph, an opera played. On one floor, Nicole heard Hitler's voice on a staticky radio mixed with the sounds of children laughing and playing behind the apartment door. When they reached the top landing, Suzanne knocked. The door opened. A young man with a cigarette hanging from his lip stood in the entrance, the old man behind him.

"Silver candlesticks were mentioned?" the young man asked.

Nicole nodded, pulled the heavy candlesticks from her coat, and gave them to him.

"You have a valise?"

She gave him that, too.

"Now wait."

Suzanne slipped inside, then the young man shut the door in Nicole's face. Liz-Bette blinked furiously, a new nervous habit. "Maybe they're stealing the candlesticks from us. Maybe we should leave."

Suddenly, the door reopened, and the young man with

the cigarette thrust the valise at Nicole. She took it, shocked at how heavy it was. "Go," he commanded, practically pushing Suzanne out before slamming the door once again.

"Come on," Suzanne urged. "Let's go!"

Quickly, they descended the stairs. "What's in the valise?" Nicole asked. "My arm feels like it is about to come out of its socket."

"Foie gras," Suzanne answered. "My grandfather's brother-in-law runs a factory in Meaux. The old man sends the factory goose liver and gets tins of foie gras in return. You now have forty half-kilo tins. I hope you like goose liver."

When they reached the street, Nicole hesitated. On the black market, the candlesticks were worth perhaps two kilos of foie gras, not twenty. "All this for two candlesticks?"

"I augmented their value a bit," Suzanne admitted. "Not very much." For ten times their worth, she must have augmented them a lot. With what? Gold coins? Diamonds? Nicole held the valise out to Suzanne. "You must take some of this."

"No," Suzanne said sharply, as she backed away from them. "I am ashamed to say what some members of my family do and who their friends are. I am not a fine enough person to refuse to benefit from their largesse. But it gives me great satisfaction to know that you are now a beneficiary, too. God bless you, Nicole." She turned and ran until her coat was a red dot in the distance.

By the time Nicole and Liz-Bette reached the Trocadéro station, it was nearly dark. Nicole had but one goal as they left the last car—to get home as quickly as possible. They were in violation of a host of anti-Jewish laws and some that applied to non-Jews as well—even though everyone did it, trafficking in the black market was a serious offense. Fortunately, the avenue de Camoëns was just a few blocks away.

"I wish I could put my coat on," Liz-Bette said, as they trudged along. "I am freezing."

"You know we can't let anyone see our stars now. Not with this valise. We'll be home in just another minute." She switched the valise to her other hand. "When Maman is better, she can trade some foie gras for other food. But she will ask what we did to get so much of it."

"Can't we just tell her the truth?"

"No, because the truth sounds unbelievable. She will be angry enough that we went out without—"

"Nicole?"

Something in Liz-Bette's voice made Nicole look up. Approaching them were two young men with black berets, not much older than Nicole. One had blond hair, the other brown. Their coats flapped open, exposing dark shirts with narrow ties. Their trousers were tucked into high black boots.

Nicole's breath caught. Permilleux Service.

The Permilleux Service was a special anti-Jewish police force created by a French government agency. It was notorious for being as sadistic as the Gestapo.

"Keep your head down, just keep walking," Nicole said softly.

The two militiamen blocked their way. "What have we here?" the blond young man asked jovially.

"Excuse us, please," Nicole said, cocking her head in the vague direction of home. "We live a few streets from here and we are late already. Come on, Liz-Bette."

"Liz-Bette. What a pretty name for a pretty girl," the other man said. "I am Antoine, and this fellow is Serge. Shall we escort you two young ladies home?"

"No!" Liz-Bette squeaked, edging closer to Nicole.

"A shame. In that case, identity cards, please." He held out a beefy hand. They had no choice. Both girls took out their identity cards, stamped JUIVE, and handed them over.

The one named Serge laughed nastily and poked his partner in the ribs. "Well, well, Antoine, we have before us two members of the chosen people trying to pass themselves off as pure French girls. Trust you to find a Jewess pretty!"

Antoine's face reddened as he glared at Nicole and Liz-Bette. "Stupid Jew cows. Trying to make a fool out of me, eh?"

"No, sir, my father has an Ausweis," Nicole explained quickly. "And we were just going—"

"What is in the valise?" He jerked it from Nicole's hand and popped it open. Tins of foie gras spilled onto the sidewalk. "Where did you get this? Did you steal it? Or is it from the black market?"

"A friend . . . gave it to us," Nicole stammered.

"No," Serge said. "You are mistaken. A friend gave it to *us*. Gather up the tins and put them back into our valise." Nicole and Liz-Bette did as what they were told, leaving the valise on the sidewalk before them.

He smiled coldly. "Now that your mysterious friend has made this lovely gift to the true defenders of pure France, there is the matter of your contravention of the Jew statute of May 1942. You are not wearing your stars. However, we may be persuaded to look the other way. There is something about which I have always been curious. I hear that Jewesses have fur all the way to their navels. A sort of animal pelt. Is it true?"

Nicole froze.

"I asked, *Is it true?*"

Nicole forced herself to speak. "No."

The dark-haired man cocked one eyebrow. "Prove it, and we shall let you go."

"Please, keep the food. Just let us go."

Suddenly, the blond one grabbed Liz-Bette by her hair, jerking her so hard that she cried out. "You have broken the law, Jew whores. Do you want to go to Drancy?" He jutted his chin at Nicole. "Lift your skirt, Mademoiselle Bernhardt. Now. Or else I will make your pretty little sister lift hers instead."

With trembling fingers, Nicole reached for the bottom of her skirt.

"What do you think, Antoine? We should be enjoying a Dubonnet with the floor show," Serge joked. "Proceed, mademoiselle."

Slowly, Nicole began to raise her skirt. Past her calves. To her knees—

An air-raid siren sounded.

Antoine cursed. "Where's the closest shelter?"

"Trocadéro," his partner said. "What about them?"

"Forget them. Let's go." The sirens wailed as Antoine grabbed the valise and ran toward Trocadéro, his partner right behind.

Nicole took Liz-Bette's hand. "Run, Liz-Bette. Run!"

They had lost everything—the candlesticks, the valise, the food—but none of that mattered now. As they reached the avenue de Camoëns, they heard the distant thunder of the Allies' bombs falling. Nicole said a silent prayer of thanks. Many times, she had prayed for the Allies to come quickly. Tonight, they had come just in time.

twenty-five

NOTES FROM GIRL X

7 January 1944

To *the people of Paris,*

Today, I give you irony. We are starving Jews who could be taken away at any moment, for any reason or no reason. Yet my parents still felt they must pun-ish LB and me for disobeying them and going to the black market. Here is the irony: What could they take from us that had not already been taken? The cinema? Cafes? Walks in the park? Evenings with friends in their homes? All are already forbidden.

So this is what our parents did—they took away our books, pens, paper, and chessboard for an entire week. You cannot imagine what it is like to be trapped in an apartment without these things. There was nothing to do but nurse Maman back to health and play the piano.

And now, for some excitement. On Day Six of our punishment, two representatives of the CGQJ paid us a visit. We were reminded that under the law of 22 July 1941, French authorities are permitted to seize Jewish property and sell it for the "benefit of France." In other words, legalized stealing. Four workmen came and took away our piano.

Dear reader, if you purchase a grand piano and find a small brass plaque on the inside etched with a Jewish name, then you, too, are a thief. Think of Girl X when you play your stolen piano. By the way, her favorite piece is Für Elise.

twenty-six

NOTES FROM GIRL X

2 March 1944

To the people of Paris!

Today, I speak to those of you who are young like me. Do you love someone with all your heart and soul, as Girl X loves J?

If you do, you will understand. I want him to undress me with more than just his eyes. I want him to touch every inch of my flesh. I burn. If you are young and in love, you know what I am feeling as I approach my seventeenth birthday. If you have forgotten, I pity you. And I think that perhaps Girl X, a Jewish girl, is freer than you are.

twenty-seven

7 April 1944

They kissed breathlessly in the hallway outside Mme. Genet's apartment. In Jacques's arms she could be anywhere, even America. She could be at a movie star's party in Hollywood, doing the jitterbug with Jacques. Everyone would say they were the best dancers there. And food! So much food that she would say, "No, thank you, no dessert for me, I couldn't bear another bite."

Too soon, Jacques ended their kiss. She buried her head against his chest, in the perfect spot just under his chin, as he stroked her cheek. "André will be home for dinner tonight. I have to go."

" 'I have to go.' Those are the ugliest words in the entire French language." She snuggled against him again. "But thank you again for bringing us wine. You cannot imagine what it means to have wine for our Passover seder tonight."

"I was happy to do it. I should be able to bring vegetables from my uncle's farm in a few days."

"When will you come back? Can you come tomorrow?"

She heard the neediness in her voice, but she couldn't seem to help herself.

"I have to study. I'll try." He kissed her again and she clung to him.

Suddenly, Mme. Genet's door swung open. "Celebrating liberation already?" she sneered. "Don't think that I am blind to you two rutting dogs. I should report you to the authorities."

Though she knew they weren't violating any laws, Nicole's face burned. She felt sure that Mme. Genet would love to denounce her family and grab whatever was left in their apartment.

Jacques stepped toward the concierge, hat in hand. "Excuse me, Madame Genet," he began politely, "but I was only saying good-bye to my girlfriend."

Mme. Genet sniffed. "A boy like you with a girl like her. It should be illegal."

"But it is not, much as your friends in the PPF would like it to be," Jacques said pleasantly. "One day, when Nicole and I become engaged, I am sure you will be amongst the first to wish us well. Unless of course you are in Berlin living in Hitler's bunker."

The concierge narrowed her eyes. "The Allies have not yet landed."

"Your Boche saviors of the Republic are losing the war, and you know it," Jacques scoffed. "Are you planning to become a Resistant of the Last Minute? I can already see you on liberation day, dancing on the Champs-Élysées, draped in the tricolor: 'Long live de Gaulle, long live freedom, long live France!' "

The concierge quivered with indignation and slammed her door shut.

Nicole jumped into Jacques's arms. "You were wonderful!"

"She is a mean-spirited fascist cow, eh?"

"Did you . . . mean what you said?"

He pretended to misunderstand. "Sadly, I do not think Mme. Genet will ever congratulate us, Nicole."

"That is not what I meant and you know it."

"Oh, you mean the 'when Nicole and I become engaged' part? But of course. Don't you remember? I asked you to marry me in third grade. I told you that one day I would become a fine doctor and practice medicine with your father. You said yes to this entire plan. It is far too late for you to back out now."

"I'll have to think about it. It's just that I have so many offers."

He tickled her ribs, which stuck out too far these days. Then he pulled her to him and kissed her until there was nothing in the world but him, his hands, his mouth, and this moment.

"Jacques . . ."

Into her neck he breathed, "Yes?"

"What you said . . . what you want . . . I want it, too."

"Someday when all of this is over, we will—"

She pulled away so that she could look into his eyes. "Not someday, Jacques. Now."

"But—"

"There is no 'someday,' don't you see?"

"Yes, there is." He tenderly touched her cheek. "Nicole—"

"Tomorrow afternoon. My mother will be out shopping and my father will be at the hospital. We can go to his study."

He pulled her to him. "I wanted our first time to be so much more than that. Candlelight and rose petals and champagne—"

"I don't care about those things," she insisted. "Don't say it isn't right, Jacques. It's the only right thing in my life." This time it was she who kissed him until there were no more words.

∽

Nicole sat on the couch; Liz-Bette at the window seat, blinking nervously. Both had resolved not to look at the grandfather clock anymore, but couldn't help themselves. It was five minutes before eight and their father was not home yet. On any other night, this would not be a great cause for concern—he could be late at the hospital, he could be on a mission. But tonight? The night different from all other nights, the sacred first night of Passover? He had assured them he would be home by seven.

Everything was ready. They were dressed in their least threadbare outfits and the table was set for the seder, the religious meal that began the eight-day Passover holiday. The precious bottle of wine Jacques had brought for them waited by her father's setting. Next to it was the ornate silver kiddush cup used only on Passover.

Mme. Bernhardt set a Haggadah—the book that retold the story of the Exodus from Egypt and contained the seder service—on each plate. As she put down the last one, the sirens that signaled the Jewish curfew began to wail.

"Maman?" Liz-Bette asked. "Where is Papa?"

"She doesn't know, Liz-Bette," Nicole said. "If she knew, we would know."

"But we can't have Passover without Papa." Liz-Bette looked desperate. "I know why you are not answering me, Maman. It is because they took Papa away on a big bus and I'm never going to see him again!"

"No," their mother said, but there was fear in her voice.

"You're lying!"

Nicole went to her. "He's safe, Liz-Bette."

"How do you know?"

"I just do."

Liz-Bette blinked rapidly. "It's true that no one came to say Nightbird."

Mme. Bernhardt finally found her voice. "Yes, I am sure that he is in a safe place, doing important work to defeat the Nazis."

Abruptly, she went to the kitchen; Nicole and Liz-Bette sat by the window, perfectly still. The only sound was the relentless ticking of the clock. Time was a thief, sneaking forward. Five minutes passed. Ten. Fifteen. Their mother returned and sat wordlessly in the upholstered chair. Twenty. Twenty-five.

The clock gonged half past eight. Mme. Bernhardt stood. "We will begin our seder," she announced.

Nicole was incredulous. "Now?"

"Passover is the festival of freedom our people have celebrated for thousands of years. Even Hitler cannot change that. Come."

The girls followed their mother to the table and opened their Haggadoth. " 'We are here to celebrate once again the very first festival the Jewish people ever observed,' " Mme. Bernhardt read aloud. " 'We retell the ancient story of how Moses led us out of Egypt and out of the house of bondage. As we remember this moving chapter in our people's past, may we learn to appreciate more deeply the freedom we now enjoy.' "

Nicole's heart hardened at the familiar words from the Haggadah. How bitter and ironic they were tonight. How could she learn to appreciate something she no longer had? What was the point of saying it?

Her mother's hand touch hers. "Nicole, so long as we say these words and have this seder, they have not defeated us. Do you understand?"

Nicole nodded. Her mother returned to the Haggadah. " 'In gratitude to God,' " she read, " 'we rise now to recite the kiddush blessing over the first of the four cups of wine.' " Mme. Bernhardt poured a tiny bit of red wine into each goblet, then stood. "Before we say the festival kiddush, we will say a special prayer for your father. Liz-Bette, will you lead us?"

"Dear God," Liz-Bette began uncertainly. "Please . . . let Papa be all right. And let him come home to us and not get taken away on a big bus forever, because . . . because . . ." Her voice cracked, and her eyes filled with tears.

"Because we love Papa as much as we love freedom," Nicole continued, "and because he is brave enough to do what is right. Amen."

"Amen," her mother and sister echoed. Nicole pretended not to see as Liz-Bette fisted the tears from her face. They raised their glasses and Mme. Bernhardt chanted the Hebrew blessings over the Passover wine. "*L'chaim*, to life," she concluded.

"*L'chaim.*" They each took the smallest sip of wine. Nicole stared at the front door, willing it to open. Her father would take off his coat and apologize profusely for arriving late on this night of nights. The metro had been running late. Someone had gotten sick at the hospital. He'd wash his hands and kiss his family and lead the seder as he always did. But the door did not open.

Mme. Bernhardt continued. " 'We have thanked God for the wine, which adds joy to life,' " she read. " 'On Pesach we thank Him especially for the precious gift of freedom. And we thank Him for—' "

She was interrupted by the pounding of feet on the stairs, followed by a fist slamming against the door to their flat. They sprang to their feet. This was the nightmare—the

Gestapo at your door to take you to Drancy. There was nowhere to run, no place to hide.

"I will go," Nicole forced herself to say. She went to the door, marveling at how if you just put one foot before the other, no matter what terror you might feel, you reached your destination anyway.

She opened the door. Standing there, disheveled and gasping for breath, was David Ginsburg. "David!" Nicole hugged him hard, giddy with joy and faint with relief. "Oh, David, you're still alive! I haven't seen you in such a long time. Are you all right? No one knew what happened to you. I am so happy to see you!" She knew she was babbling but she didn't care. She tugged him into the apartment. "Come join our seder!"

He would not move. "David?" Nicole asked. "David?"

Finally, he spoke one word. "Nightbird."

twenty-eight

NOTES FROM GIRL X

14 April 1944

To the people of Paris,

Greetings from Girl X and her family, now in hiding. They can shut me away, but they cannot shut down my voice. The proof is in your hands. Read this, then pass it on.

As this missive could easily get in the hands of the Boche, I must be extraordinarily careful to say nothing about our location. Suffice to say that it is big enough to hold a Jewish family that would rather hide like mice in the wall than allow themselves to be deported.

The place is tiny. I cannot go more than nine paces in any direction without banging into a wall. At one point the wall slopes inward, so you have to duck to get under it. This is the nook where I have decided to sleep, next to LB.

Monsieur L gave us two valises when we arrived.

In them was food, four blankets, some candles and matches, and a table setting. There is one bedraggled chair that bites you with its sharp springs. That is it. Oh yes, our bathroom: a bucket covered with a tight lid.

J and M know where we are. J is the boy I love. M is my best friend. They bring us food. Thank God for that. M also smuggles out these Notes from Girl X.

On Passover we were warned by D to flee from our apartment. He said nothing more no matter how much we begged. We knew what to do, correct? He did not wait for us to leave, but ran downstairs immediately. D got word to J and M about where we were. A miracle.

We fled, wearing layers of clothes, carrying nothing. I took one journal in my waistband and some ink and pens in a pocket. We crossed Paris praying no patrol would stop us. When we arrived here, Monsieur L was waiting. He led us to our hiding place.

Papa returned to us forty-eight hours later. It was the happiest moment of my life. But he still goes out at night. Sometimes to do Resistance work, sometimes to look for food and water. We have practically none. Every time he leaves, I am so afraid for him.

We have one window, covered with old newspaper. I fashioned newspaper chess pieces, then drew a chessboard on the floor. LB and I play game after game to pass the time. Other than that, there is nothing to do but pray for the Allied invasion. J and M bring us war news. The Allies bombed near Normandy. Perhaps that is where the invasion will come. What are they waiting for?

And now I shall write about love. On Passover we say: Why on this night do we eat bitter herbs? On the eve of Passover, I made a decision that J and I would make love for the very first time the next afternoon. I felt so strong. How could I know that the very next afternoon I would be here, shut away from everyone and everything? If only I had told him sooner, even one day sooner, it would have happened. Now J and I can never be alone. Passover ends tomorrow. But the bitter taste in my mouth won't end with it. I still don't know what it's like to be completely his, in every way. I don't feel powerful anymore. Is this the Huns' victory? How mighty they must feel, then, to have robbed me of my dreams.

twenty-nine

NOTES FROM GIRL X

1 June 1944

To the people of Paris,
   To be in hiding is boring. And yet I am always tense. I think about J all the time. Even when he is here he is like vapor, escaping through the cracks until he is entirely gone again. To be with him but never to have privacy is torture. Sometimes we sneak a kiss. Maman pretends not to see. We can go no further. It makes me want to scream. J weaves fantasies for me that always begin, "After liberation . . ." Yesterday he said, "After liberation we will stay in the finest hotel in Paris, drink champagne, eat caviar, and make love once for every night we missed during the war." When he says such things, I close my eyes, and for just a moment, I believe him. But when I open them, I am the same filthy girl stuck in the same filthy place. I have not had a bath in almost two months. I cannot wash my clothes. I know I smell

wretched, because sometimes I get close to the cov-
ered window and put my nose by a crack in the
glass, where I can breathe in air from outside. When
I move away from the glass, I am nearly asphyxiated.
I reek, we all reek. Yet J says nothing about this. He
simply continues to weave magical spells that begin,
"After liberation . . . "

But . . . how can he love me when I am like this?
How?

thirty

NOTES FROM GIRL X

8 June 1944

To the people of Paris,
   The invasion of France has come, and the Allies are fighting their way east from Normandy! Girl X hides in a Left Bank attic with her Jewish family. She is hungry, she is filthy, but she lives. She believes with all her heart that the Huns will be defeated and she will dance in the sunshine of her beloved Paris once more. God bless General Eisenhower. God bless General Montgomery. We will be free!

thirty-one

18 June 1944

Nicole? Are you awake?"

"No."

"I have a question about Scarlett O'Hara."

"I'm sleeping, Liz-Bette. Leave me alone." Nicole was in a terrible mood. So what if the Allies had invaded France? They were nowhere near Paris. Her own situation hadn't altered at all.

Liz-Bette raised herself up on one bony elbow, blinking rapidly. "How can I leave you alone, Nicole? There is no other place to go."

"You are such a pest." Nicole turned over. "Well? What is your burning question about Scarlett O'Hara?"

"Just this," Liz-Bette said, all seriousness. "Did she dance as well as you?"

Nicole instantly regretted having taken out her frustration on her little sister. Things were not easy for her, either. She brushed some hair from Liz-Bette's cheek. "She danced better than me. Scarlett was the most wonderful dancer in all of the state of Georgia."

"Scar-lett," Liz-Bette said dreamily. "Such a beautiful name. After liberation I shall change my name to Scar-lett. I hate the name Liz-Bette. It sounds terribly childish."

"All right, Scar-lett," Nicole declared. "If you want to be known as Scar-lett, Scar-lett you will be."

Liz-Bette grinned. "I will have beautiful ball gowns like Scar-lett had before the War Between the States."

"A different one for every dance," Nicole embellished. "Because a magnificent beauty like Scar-lett Bernhardt cannot possibly be seen in the same gown twice."

"The first one will be blue, to match my eyes," Liz-Bette decided, as she cuddled up next to Nicole. "Boys like you if you can dance, right?"

"Sometimes."

"Will you teach me to dance when we get home?"

"Absolutely."

"I want to learn how to jitterbug, where the boy flips you and your skirt flies into the air."

Nicole laughed. "Scarlett O'Hara did not jitterbug. You want your skirt to fly into the air?"

"I will wear very beautiful silk lingerie underneath," Liz-Bette explained. "Why wear beautiful lingerie if no one but you sees it?"

"Excellent point."

Liz-Bette yawned. "Do you think this is the night that the Gestapo will come?"

"No."

"What will they do to us if they catch us?"

"We will go to Drancy. And then to a work camp, I suppose."

"Will we all still be together?"

"I hope so."

"Promise?" Liz-Bette asked sleepily.

"I can't promise because I don't know."

"Promise anyway." Liz-Bette's eyes drooped shut.

Nicole took in her sister's tiny frame. The idea that the Boche would have any use for a girl with no strength to work was incomprehensible. "I promise," she whispered. "Now sleep."

There was soft knocking on the attic door—three fast raps, silence, then two more. Mme. Bernhardt awoke with a start. "It's okay, Maman," Nicole assured her, as she scrambled to her feet. "It's Jacques, I'm sure." She pulled the door open. Jacques entered. He and Nicole clung to each other.

"I brought food," he said quietly. "I am sorry. It is only potatoes and apples."

"It is food, thank you." Mme. Bernhardt took the mesh bag from Jacques. "Liz-Bette, come over here, please, and give them some privacy."

Liz-Bette sighed dramatically as she went to her mother. "I can still hear every word they say, you know."

"Well, pretend you cannot," Mme. Bernhardt said. "It is called discretion, and it is very French."

Nicole and Jacques moved into Nicole's nook and sat facing the wall. "I missed you so much," she whispered, wrapping her arms around his neck.

"I feel the same." He gently pulled her hands away. "Where is your father?"

"Trying to find us food," Nicole lied.

"I wish he wouldn't go out at night, Nicole. I will bring more food so—"

"Shhh." She put her finger to his lips. "No talk of food. It only makes me hungry." She replaced her finger with her lips, kissing him softly.

His mind was clearly elsewhere. "It's just that it is so dangerous, Nicole. Do you want to hear some shocking news? Ten days ago some resistants exploded a railway bridge near Limoges."

She nodded emphatically. "Good."

"Good?" Jacques was incredulous. "You will not say that when you hear what the Boche did in reprisal."

"What?"

"They picked out a small village nearby, completely unconnected to the Resistance, a place with hardly any Jews. They waited for the day the cigarette ration would be distributed, because hundreds of people would be coming from the countryside. They surrounded this village. They shot the men, put the women and children in the church and burned them alive. Then they burned down the entire town. Now there is no more Oradour-sur-Glane."

Nicole gasped. "Where?"

"Oradour-sur-Glane. You know it?"

Life is fine in Oradour-sur-Glane. I am planning my wedding . . .

The postcard from Claire Einhorn. Nicole had read it again and again.

Should we serve smoked salmon or roast chicken?

"Nicole?" Jacques touched her arm.

"I knew someone there."

"I'm sorry. Who?"

"It doesn't matter." Cold fury welled up in Nicole—at Claire's death, at the Boche, at day after day of being afraid, filthy, and hungry, hidden away in an attic. And there was Jacques. Clean. And free. No. He could never understand.

"How dare you condemn the Resistance?" she hissed at him, wanting—needing—someone to blame. "They did not burn Oradour. They are risking their lives fighting Hitler."

"And I am risking my life, too, every time I bring you food!"

"So, don't come then!"

They stared at each other, hearts racing, across some nameless abyss that neither could cross, faces barely visible in the dim attic light. Nicole wished she could take her stupid, prideful words and stuff them back into her mouth.

Jacques exhaled slowly. "Be as obstinate as you want, Nicole. I will still come." He took her hand. "Because I say yes to hiding people I love. But to attack well-armed Nazis with homemade bottle bombs? This is not resistance. This is insanity."

"No." She wrenched her hand from his. "You are wrong. People must rise up and fight until France is free—"

"Stop it!" He grabbed her roughly by the shoulders. "Don't you understand? France will be free, but you'll all be dead!"

Horrified, she pulled away.

"Nicole, please," he whispered, his voice tortured, "I would give my life for you." His hand found hers again in the dim light. "I will find a way to get you more food. But please, please tell your father not to leave your hiding place. If he's caught, they will think he's a resistant. They won't just deport him, Nicole. They'll kill him."

∽

Hours later, Nicole snapped awake at the creak of the attic door. She fumbled for the matches, lighting one. Her father stood in the doorway. He looked exhausted.

"Go back to sleep, little one," he whispered. "It is late."

Nicole shook her head and lit a candle stub. "Jacques brought food."

"Good." He sat heavily and removed his shoes. Nicole glanced at her mother and sister. They were snoring together on Maman's blanket.

"Papa . . . did you hear about the massacre at Oradour-sur-Glane?"

"Yes."

"Claire Einhorn was there."

Her father looked pained. "Yes," he said finally. "I remember now."

Nicole didn't know what to say, so she rested her head on her father's lap. "Do you think the Allies will reach Paris very soon, Papa?"

"By the end of July. August, perhaps."

"Can't you just wait, then? We are all still together. If you would only stop now we will still be together and alive when the Americans come. And then—"

"No."

Nicole sat up. "What is it, Papa? Is the fight more important than we are? Is it?"

"How can you possibly understand?" Dr. Bernhardt struggled to find the right words. "Once I put my trust in other men, Nicole. To protect me, my family, our people. God, I was such a fool."

"Don't say that."

"I was a fool," he repeated. "And a coward. I did not want to believe that such terrible things could happen. Now I will never trust someone else to fight my fight again. Not France, not the Allies, not anyone."

"But it will all be over soon. It has to be."

"Does it? This is an enemy who rounds us up instead of committing every man to the fight. That is how deeply they hate, Nicole. It does not stop just because the Allies are on French soil."

"So you throw bottle bombs on a public street? What

good does it do?" she cried in frustration. "Do something that matters. Go free the Jews in Drancy!"

"And where would we get the gasoline to get to Drancy? We have no fuel, no food, no money. We are invisible soldiers of the night, and we do what we can."

"If they catch you, Papa, they'll kill you." Her eyes searched his. "I know it is a war. And I know how selfish I am. But I would rather we go to a work camp than die."

"A concentration camp is not just a work camp, Nicole."

She was taken aback. "What is it, then?"

Her father didn't answer. Instead, he went to the window, peering through the sliver of cracked glass under the newspaper at the bottom. "It is amazing, isn't it?" he said softly. "The same stars and the same moon just keep shining. Terrible things happen, things too awful to even believe. But the stars keep shining just the same."

"What terrible things, Papa?"

With infinite tenderness he enveloped Nicole in his arms. "Go to sleep, little one," he said. "Dream about the stars."

thirty-two

25 July 1944

Nicole stared at a miracle: six pastries. Two lemon tarts, two napoleons, and two éclairs. Mimi had attended a party on the Île Saint-Louis the night before, in honor of the opening of Monique's latest play. She had managed to sneak the pastries out of the party in a discarded cigar box.

"Go ahead," Mimi urged. "The Allies are coming at any moment. We will start our celebration early."

Liz-Bette coughed fitfully, eyeing the pastries. She had a respiratory infection that she seemed unable to shake. "But if I eat even one, it will be gone forever."

Her mother held up an éclair. "Eat, darling."

Her darkly circled eyes grew huge as she took a bite. "Oh, Maman, it is so good!"

Mme. Bernhardt nodded and put one lemon tart aside. "We will save this for your father."

Nicole bit into the remaining tart. The taste was amazing—sugar and flour and butter, and the soft lemony center stinging her tongue. "Astonishing," she rhapsodized. "This is the most delicious thing I ever tasted in my life."

"I'm happy to have liberated them from the enemy," Mimi said proudly.

"Tell us more about the party, Mimi," Nicole urged. "Jacques was the handsomest boy there, right?"

"If you say so."

"Did he dance with a lot of pretty girls?"

"Only with Monique and Maman and me," Mimi assured her. "But the party was completely decadent. The Boche pig ambassador was there. There was champagne, and real coffee—"

"Real coffee," Mme. Bernhardt echoed wistfully. "To taste real coffee."

"Maybe Mimi can steal that for you, too, Maman," Liz-Bette joked, her eyes fixed on the napoleons. Her mother pushed one in her direction. She snatched it up and took a big bite.

"Liz-Bette, I must tell you about the most embarrassing thing that happened to me at the party," Mimi said, clearly seeking to distract the girl from the fact that two small pastries could not begin to satisfy her hunger.

"What?" Liz-Bette mumbled through her chewing.

"Well, it was a very formal event. Since I did not happen to have a spare ball gown, my mother decided to sew me one from the drapes in our kitchen. How humiliating! It was much too big in the bosom. She said I would grow into it. Ha."

"That's all right," Liz-Bette commiserated. "I don't think I'll ever get a bosom, either."

"So," Mimi continued, "I stuffed myself with socks to make it look as if I had a bosom. And when Monique's brother asked me to dance, the socks fell out, right in the middle of the dance floor!"

Liz-Bette shrieked with laughter. "What did you do?"

"I stepped right over them and kept on dancing."

Mme. Bernhardt applauded. "Good for you, Mimi."

"Dancing," Nicole said wistfully. She gazed at the newspaper-covered window as if she could see through it, all the way to a fancy theater party. "I miss dancing."

"When all of this is over, you and I shall go dancing every night," Mimi declared. "We will have sexy high heels with leather soles—"

"And real silk stockings—" Nicole added.

"With seams," Liz-Bette put in.

"We'll dance and dance and dance," Nicole murmured. She closed her eyes, hearing music in her head. "I will be in Jacques's arms—"

"And I will be with a handsome Resistance fighter," Mimi said.

Liz-Bette flung her arms wide. "And I will be with Clark Gable!"

They all laughed, then Liz-Bette began to cough again. Her mother rubbed her back until she could catch her breath. There were no workers downstairs at this hour, so Nicole didn't worry so much about the noise. But she did worry about her sister's cough, which seemed to worsen every day.

"Do you know what I saw today on avenue Foch?" Mimi asked. "Some wart-faced Huns packing documents into a lorry. They looked so nervous. It was wonderful. The Occupation really is almost over."

Nicole nodded. "Papa says a month at the most."

Liz-Bette fingered her filthy hair. "Maman, do you think my hair will ever get pretty again?"

"I am certain of it."

"In that case, after the war, I want it styled like Hedy Lamarr."

Mimi chucked Liz-Bette under the chin. "Liz-Bette, you will be a devastating beauty, breaking the heart of every young man in Paris. And if you still want to be editor of *For Her*, you shall be that, too."

Liz-Bette nodded. "Most likely."

Mimi checked her watch. "I have to go. I am supposed to meet my brothers in ten minutes. André is on duty near here. He wants us to try to catch our dinner in the Seine. Can you picture me reeling in a fish?" She shook her head at the ridiculousness of the concept. "But Jacques says that I must help, it increases our chances. My brothers are maddening." She reached for Nicole's hand to pull her friend to her feet. "Promise me that when you two are married, you won't let him boss you around."

"There is no chance of that," Nicole assured her. "Maman, excuse us a moment."

"Of course. Liz-Bette, come sit with me."

Liz-Bette shuffled over to her mother as Nicole and Mimi

crawled into the recesses of the nook, their backs turned to the others. Nicole slipped a hand into her pocket and passed Mimi the latest edition of *Notes from Girl X*; Mimi hid it under the waistband of her skirt. "Perhaps the Allied paratroopers will arrive tonight and this will be your last one," Mimi whispered.

"I hope so."

Liz-Bette's voice rang out. "What are you two doing?"

"It's private," Nicole called back.

"That is extremely rude," Liz-Bette said.

Mimi kissed Nicole on each cheek. "I will see you soon."

"Give Jacques a big kiss from me."

"Why anyone would want to kiss my brother is beyond me, so I will let you deliver that message yourself. Liz-Bette?"

"Yes?"

Mimi went to her. "Next time I come, you and I will have a secret discussion, eh?" Liz-Bette nodded and Mimi kissed her good-bye.

"Be careful that no one sees you leave, Mimi," Mme. Bernhardt warned.

Mimi grinned. "I will be like the Lone Ranger and ride on the wind."

Nicole watched Mimi disappear out the secret half-door, aching to follow her. She could so easily picture the two of them walking on the rue de Passy, stopping in Alain's cafe, going to the movies. Or just being together in her room in the apartment on avenue de Camoëns. How wonderful it would be to be back home again, to sleep in her own bed.

How wonderful simply to open her window on a July morning.

"I wish I could go with her." Liz-Bette's voice was small. Nicole turned. Her sister was staring at the half-door, blinking.

"Me, too," Nicole admitted. "She's meeting Jacques. I miss him so much. Even when he's here, I miss him. I know that sounds stupid."

Liz-Bette spun around crazily and then dropped to her knees. "Oh, Jacques, Jacques. I love you so." She imitated Nicole, kissing up and down her own skinny arms. "I want to smooch you all over!"

"Shhh," Nicole cautioned, because their mother was already snoring softly. They sat in the nook.

"Nicole? What is it like, to kiss a boy?"

Nicole smiled. "Wonderful."

Liz-Bette put her head in Nicole's lap. "But what if . . . promise you won't laugh?"

"I promise."

"What if—by mistake—you spit in his mouth?"

Nicole bit her lip to keep from laughing. "I have never heard of a girl spitting into a boy's mouth before, so I don't think you have to worry."

Liz-Bette looked up, worry lines creasing her forehead. "I could be the first."

"Practice on the back of your hand."

Liz-Bette looked dubious. "Really?"

"It's what I did."

Liz-Bette held her hand out, then moved it close to her lips. "Oh, Clark, we mustn't let your past, or your mustache, come between us." As she began to smother her hand with kisses, her body was wracked by coughs.

"Why don't you rest, Liz-Bette?" Nicole asked. "You need to get rid of that cough in time for liberation."

"All I do is rest." Liz-Bette pouted, but she stretched out on the blanket. "Don't cover me. It is far too hot in here already."

She was right. The attic was hot. Stifling, in fact. "All right, no blanket," Nicole agreed. "But close your eyes."

"I don't want to close my eyes."

"You have a very obstinate nature, Liz-Bette."

"You don't get to tell me what to do. You are not my mother."

Frustration welled up inside Nicole. Suddenly, she could not stand it one moment longer—the sameness, fear, hunger, heat, and filth. She didn't care if the Allies were arriving in an hour or a day or a lifetime. She had to have five minutes in the open air, to breathe like a human being, or else she was sure she would lose her mind.

"Liz-Bette?"

"What?"

"I am going to tell you a secret. You must promise never to tell Maman or Papa."

"What?"

"Promise first."

"I promise. What?"

Nicole glanced at her mother, to make sure she was asleep, then leaned close to her sister. "I am going up on the roof."

"*What?*" Liz-Bette sat up quickly.

"Shhh! There's a ladder to it. And a trapdoor at the top. I will be gone for five minutes only."

"I'm coming, too."

"No. And don't say I'm not your mother, either. What if you started coughing up there and someone heard you?"

It was a long moment before Liz-Bette spoke. "I admit you are right. But I remember what Paris smells like in summer. Like flowers."

"I wish I could bottle the air for you, but I can't."

"No," Liz Bette agreed sadly. "You can't."

Nicole put a finger to her lips, reminding Liz-Bette to be silent, then tiptoed to the half-door and opened it. There was the ladder. She climbed it rung by rung until she reached the top. There was the trapdoor. She pushed. It opened easily. And she was outside.

The fresh air tasted like champagne. She climbed out and sprawled on her back, inhaling, exhaling, swimming in the deliciousness of it. She wished she could tear off her disgusting clothes and fling them from the building, to let the clean air touch her everywhere.

Giddy with oxygen, she crawled to the building's edge and looked down. Though the light was fading, Nicole could make out people walking on the street, people on bicycles, all going somewhere. It would be so wonderful, she thought, just to be going somewhere.

Behind her on the roof, there was a loud noise. Her heart lurched. She lay still, not daring to look.

"Nicole?"

Maddening! She should have known Liz-Bette wouldn't listen. Nicole stabbed the air with her index finger in the direction of the trapdoor, meaning that Liz-Bette should go back this instant. But her sister ignored her and strolled over as if she were walking in the Luxembourg gardens.

"Crawl," Nicole hissed. Liz-Bette dropped to her hands and knees. Nicole held up two fingers, meaning Liz-Bette could stay on the roof for two minutes. Her sister held up five in response, negotiating for extra time. Already, she was edging close to the parapet wall of the building, to look at the street below. Nicole was about to drag her backwards when they were both startled by the sound of three quick explosions. They froze.

Moments later, sharp gunfire echoed in the streets. "It's the Allies!" Liz-Bette cried.

Nicole didn't think so. She crawled to the building's edge, Liz-Bette beside her, and looked to her left, where she thought the sound had originated. Yes! There, at the metro station entrance, a fire raged. Suddenly, she saw flashes of gunfire.

"It's the Resistance," Nicole marveled.

"Die, lousy Huns!" Liz-Bette uttered fiercely. The sisters

watched, transfixed, as the fire in the metro entrance intensified.

"I love you, whoever you are," Liz-Bette whispered. Sirens sounded. They had to get off the roof. If their mother awoke, she'd have a heart attack. Nicole cocked her head toward the trapdoor. They didn't speak again until they were safely in the hiding place. Thankfully, their mother was still snoring.

"Oh, I am so happy!" Liz-Bette hugged Nicole as sirens wailed on the street. This time, though, the sirens meant something terrible for their tormentors instead of for them. "Nicole, what do you think they were attack—"

She was interrupted by three hard raps on the half-door, silence, then two more raps. The code knock.

Nicole hurried to the door as Mme. Bernhardt jerked awake. "Who's there?" she demanded.

Mimi fell into the room, breathless. "Quick, you have to leave!"

A fist clutched Nicole's heart. "What is it?"

"They threw bottle bombs in the metro, at the Permilleux Service. It was an ambush!"

"So why—"

"André was on duty, that's where we were meeting him. My brother is dead!"

"No!" Nicole's hands flew to her mouth.

"It was your father!"

"Oh, God." Nicole reached for Mimi. "It wasn't meant for your brother—"

Mimi pushed her away, wild-eyed. "But it killed him anyway! I saw it all, they attacked from the back, they didn't know André was there. Your father was shot, he couldn't get away."

"No," Nicole insisted, as if denying it could make it not be true.

"Jacques saw, too! He was in shock, he didn't mean to, he yelled at your father, 'I loved you, I brought you food, and you killed my brother!' "

"Please God, no," Nicole moaned. "Please don't let it be—"

"You have to leave!" Mimi grabbed Nicole. "They'll torture Jacques until he tells where you are. Run!"

"I am so sorry—"

"Leave now!" Mimi whipped around to Mme. Bernhardt, who stood in mute shock. "Don't you hear me, leave—"

The pounding of a dozen jackboots on the stairs leading to the attic, and screams of guttural German, cut her off.

"Raus! Juden! Raus! Raus!"

The half-door to the hiding place was smashed open. Liz-Bette screamed and leaped into her mother's arms. Mimi and Nicole clung to each other, heart to heart, and waited for the end.

thirty-three

NOTES FROM GIRL X

17 August 1944

To the finder of this paper,
*I am Girl X. Seventeen. Jewish. Parisian. Still
alive. We continue to hear the rumble of the Allied
artillery. Liberation is upon us. Yet my sister and I
are not at the gates of Paris to greet the Americans.
Instead, we are prisoners here at Drancy.*

*More than three weeks here, now. We are alone.
Maman was deported on the convoy of 31 July. We
are part of a group of about 1,500 people still in the
camp. We hear there will be no more deportations.
What will this mean for us? Will Brunner order his
men to shoot us before he runs from the Allies?*

*I try not to think about my parents, or J, or M. My
sister is very sick, coughing constantly, jaundiced. I
made a vow to God that I will protect her, and I will.
She is asleep in the barracks. I am sitting outside*

writing this very small, to save paper. I was unable to take my journal when the Gestapo came for us. But the miracle is, today I found a pencil stub, and there is paper blowing everywhere. Why do I keep writing Notes from Girl X? There is no M to smuggle them out to the streets of Paris. It is most likely pointless. But I will push my notes into the cracks of the walls here as if I were writing to Hashem at the Wailing Wall in Jerusalem. Perhaps someone, someday, will find my notes. If you do find this at some future date, let it be recorded that Girl X was here. She lived. She loved to dance. She loved a boy.

There was no more room on the scrap of brown paper. Nicole folded it four times, pressing the creases together. Then, she walked along the wall of the barracks, looking for a crack in the concrete. She found one, and worked her note into the crevice until it disappeared. She'd hidden another scrap of paper under a rock. She took it out, brushed the dirt from its surface, and began to write again.

Drancy is a half-finished apartment complex ringed by barbed wire. We sleep on lice-infested straw. We itch constantly. I pick lice from my sister and crush them with my fingers, but it does no good. They are like the enemy—for every one I kill, they send one hundred more.

There are quite a few Resistance fighters among the remaining prisoners. They have managed to smuggle in some food. One of them is my old friend D. He was beaten and is barely recognizable. He tries to talk but his jaw is so swollen I cannot understand him.

Sometimes I wander around. It is something to do. Over the past few years many people wrote graffiti on the buildings before they were deported. I think I have read them all, memorized many. Even if the Boche bulldoze everything, they cannot bulldoze my mind, so their messages will not be lost. I will speak their names and deliver their messages.

BERNARD FRAJDENRAICH AND HIS BROTHER DIDIER, ARRESTED THE 16 JULY 1942, DEPORTED THE 25 SEPTEMBER 1942, IN VERY GOOD SPIRITS, AND WITH THE HOPES OF RETURNING VERY, VERY SOON.

SERGE AND MONIQUE PREIGHER-NEUMANN, AND THEIR MOTHER HILDA, DEPORTED THE 7 DECEMBER 1943, IN VERY GOOD SPIRITS.

To my surprise, I saw a message from someone I knew.

TZIPPORA EINHORN, ARRIVED THE 21 JULY 1942, DEPORTED THE 14 AUGUST 1942, DAUGHTER-IN-LAW OF GENIA EINHORN (DIED THE 7 AUGUST 1942).

My friend's mother had written this. I traced her
writing with my fingers over it and prayed.

Dear reader, for so long I have written anonymously,
known only as Girl X, to protect me and my loved
ones should my missive fall into enemy hands. It
occurs to me in just this moment that I can record
my name here at last. This paper, too, I will stuff into
a crack in the wall. If that is where you have found
it, dear reader, let it be recorded that one Jewish
French girl, age seventeen, by the name of

"Mademoiselle, what are you writing?"

Nicole jumped to her feet and froze. Alois Brunner, who was in charge of the Drancy camp, stood over her, flanked by two SS aides. A small, mercurial man with sharp features, Brunner always wore leather gloves with his uniform. She'd heard it was because he feared touching Jewish skin with his naked hands.

"Attention, Jew-Swine!" he bellowed. "I asked you a question!"

"Just scribbling, Herr Hauptsturmführer."

Brunner joined his gloved hands together. "Your name, Jew-Swine?"

"Bernhardt, Nicole."

"Any relation to the famous Dr. Jean Bernhardt of the Rothschild Hospital?"

"I am his daughter, Herr Hauptsturmführer."

"I met your father once at his hospital." Brunner's voice became conversational. "Do you know where he is?"

"No, Herr Hauptsturmführer."

"A pity he deserted you." Brunner thought a moment. "Your father was of course acquainted with M. Armand Kohn, correct?"

"Yes, Herr Hauptsturmführer." M. Kohn had been in charge of the entire Rothschild Hospital. Her father had spoken of him many times.

"Jew-Swine Kohn is here with the rest of his family. He is not so high and mighty anymore, I assure you." Brunner's lip curled in a half smile. He jutted his chin toward one of his aides. "Give him your paper."

Nicole hesitated.

"Are you deaf? I said give it to him!"

Nicole handed the sheet to the SS man, who held it between forefinger and thumb as if it were diseased. "Burn it," Brunner commanded. The aide took a mechanical lighter and held it to the paper. When flames began to lick his fingers, he dropped it and ground it to ash under his boot. Nicole stared ahead, her face betraying nothing.

"Daughter of Jew-Swine Dr. Jean Bernhardt, you are here with your sister, correct?"

"Yes, Herr Hauptsturmführer."

"Find your sister and present yourselves at my offices in fifteen minutes," Brunner said, his tone pleasant once more. "You are going on a journey together."

෴

I have neither paper nor pencil but I keep recording things in my mind. Brunner took fifty of us in a lorry to Paris-Bobigny station, even as Allied fighters flew overhead. They put us near the end of a Nazi troop train, in a car designed to carry military supplies. There are no seats. It is hot. We have a bucket of water to drink and another bucket to use as a commode. Liz-Bette and I have staked out one corner of the car, near Armand Kohn and his family. The train is heading east. Where, I have no idea.

ᔕ

The brakes screeched and Nicole opened her eyes. What time was it? She could barely tell; so little light penetrated the two barred windows of the car. She thought it must be early evening.

"Why do they stop and start so much, Nicole?" Liz-Bette asked hoarsely.

"I don't know." Nicole touched Liz-Bette's feverish forehead. "Lean against me and try to sleep."

As the train sped up again, Nicole looked around. Most of the other prisoners were dozing. They ranged from well-groomed Armand Kohn and his family to a few disheveled Resistance fighters. One of them was David Ginsburg. He was sleeping.

The whole transport was bizarre. They had been loaded quickly and there had been no body searches. So the resistants had been able to smuggle in bread, chocolate, and cigarettes, which they shared. Then, to Nicole's shock, they extracted tools and a tiny saw from inside their bread loaves and began to plan an escape.

This had caused a huge ruckus. They'd been repeatedly warned that in the event of an escape attempt, not only would the captured escapees be shot, so would anyone left behind on the train. M. Kohn had been irate—how dare they propose an escape that would put those who could not jump in danger? What about the little Bernhardt girl, for example? The sick one?

The resistants had been undeterred, and decided to saw a hole in the car's side wall, working only by night.

It was brightening a bit inside the car, which meant that it must be morning. Nicole rubbed her stiff neck. Incredibly, M. Kohn began shaving himself with a straight razor as if it was a normal morning at home.

"Make sure to get every whisker, Kohn," a resistant named Claude sneered. "When the SS comes again, they will certainly appreciate a stinking, clean-shaven Jew like you more than a stinking, unshaven Jew like me."

"Now, now, Claude, Herr Kohn is not yet comfortable traveling with the proletariat," a female comrade declared.

"Pay no attention to their talk of escape," M. Kohn instructed his four children. "It is an absurdity that will get us all killed."

"Stupid bourgeois Jew. Let them think for themselves. Kohn the Younger!" Claude called out to Philippe, M. Kohn's eldest son. "Did you read what Brunner scrawled on our car? JEWISH TERRORISTS. You are one of us now, eh?"

"Leave my son alone," M. Kohn demanded, which only made Claude and his friends laugh.

Nicole leaned toward Philippe. "Why do they dislike your father so much?"

"To them, bourgeois Jews like my father, who stayed in Paris and worked under the UGIF, are not much better than the Gestapo."

"But that is not fair. What were sick Jews supposed to do? Where were they supposed to go? My father—" She stopped herself. It was the first time she had said the words *my father* since that horrible night in July.

"Your father what?" Philippe asked.

Nicole leaned back against the wall of the car. "Never mind," she said.

∽

The train rumbled on. When Liz-Bette awoke, Nicole gave her a piece of bread she had saved. Liz-Bette ate half, then fell back asleep. *It is night again,* Nicole recorded in her mind, visualizing the words in fiery streaks against the insides of her eyelids. *Sometimes we stop for hours. At least when we are moving there is a little air.*

She felt a touch on her arm. "Let me sleep, Liz-Bette," she murmured.

"Nicole?"

The voice was not her sister's. It was David. There was so little light in the car she could barely make out his face.

"How are you feeling?" she asked.

"I think they broke my jaw." He winced. "But I plan to live."

"Good."

"How is Liz-Bette?"

"Sick." Nicole looked at her sister, curled up in the corner of the car. "But she plans to live, too." Their bodies vibrated as the train rumbled over an uneven section of rail bed. "David?"

"Yes?"

"The night we were arrested—do you know what happened? The night my fath—" Nicole faltered.

"The Resistance staged an ambush. Three officers in the Permilleux Service. Every evening at eight-fifteen, they came out of that metro stop."

"Were they killed?"

"Yes."

"Good." She took a ragged breath. "Do you know what happened to my father?"

David hesitated. "I understand he was badly wounded. The Gestapo took him."

He didn't need to tell her what that meant. Her father was dead.

"How did you get caught?"

David shrugged. "Completely unrelated. I was carrying a bundle of false identity papers. When I arrived at my destination, the militia answered the door. Someone tipped them off."

Liz-Bette coughed in her sleep, then rolled over and began to snore. Nicole lowered her voice. "Thank you for telling me about my father, David."

"He was a hero."

"Yes. Did they shoot Jacques, too?"

"Yes. After he betrayed you."

"No. It was an accident, he didn't mean to. His brother was dead—"

"Sometimes in a war, innocent people die." David's tone was cold. "Jacques betrayed you."

"You don't understand. He kept us alive—"

"And *then* he betrayed you. I knew he would, eventually."

What could she say? What was the truth? She didn't know anymore. From across the car, they could hear the sounds of sawing as the resistants proceeded with their plan.

"Where do you think we are?" Nicole finally asked.

"Someone boosted Claude up to the window before. He saw a sign for Bar-le-Duc."

Nicole was stunned. "That means we're still in France."

"They do not seem to be in a big hurry to get us wherever it is we're going."

"To a work camp, I hear," she said.

For a long moment, the only sound was the steady sawing on the wall.

She could feel David's eyes on her. "The hole is almost ready, Nicole."

217

She shook her head. "It's too dangerous. There must be SS on the roof with machine guns. As soon as you jump, they'll kill you."

"They'll kill us all anyway."

"That's not true. We're going to a work camp—"

"It is not a work camp," David hissed. "That's just what they say to keep us from rioting. They are killing all the Jews."

"No. That is propaganda. A lie!" She felt like hitting him for saying such a terrible thing.

"It's true," he insisted. "Listen to me, Nicole. Everyone is either shot or marched into a big room—for a shower, they'll tell you—but it isn't water that comes out of the spigots, it's gas."

"That's crazy!"

"Everyone dies, Nicole. Men, women, children—"

She put her hands over her ears. "Stop it, stop it, it's not true—"

"We've had reports from eyewitnesses—"

"They're lying."

"They're telling the truth." He pulled her hands from her ears. "It is just such a horrible truth that no one will believe it until it's too late."

She couldn't speak. What if— No. It was impossible.

"Listen to me, Nicole. The hole is almost done. We will crawl out, straddle the side, then jump. It has been raining. The ground will be soft."

"You'll die."

"Maybe. But at least they won't have had the satisfaction of killing us. Jump with me."

"I can't."

"You can."

"Even if I believed you, I can't leave Liz-Bette. She's too sick to—"

"I want you to live, Nicole!"

"God, don't you think I want that, too? But I won't leave my sister."

The sawing stopped. "We are almost ready," Claude announced.

David looked at Nicole with questioning eyes. She shook her head again, then put a hand on her sister's forehead. It still blazed with fever. "I understand," he said.

"I'll pray for you, David."

"To who? God? He must be on vacation. And He doesn't seem to have appointed a deputy while He's away."

There was a loud crash as Claude and his comrades pulled away a section of the wall and dropped it on the floor of the car. A cheer went up. Fresh air poured in, filling Nicole with longing. For the briefest moment, she allowed herself to think that perhaps she could jump, with Liz-Bette in her arms, and—

No. It was impossible. Liz-Bette would die.

"David, come. Everyone who is jumping, come!" Claude called. People headed for the escape hatch. Already the first person was climbing through the hole.

"You'll get away, David," Nicole told him. "You will live."

219

"And I'll go to Palestine."

"Palestine? What is in Palestine?"

"Nothing." Lights twinkled outside, as they passed a farmhouse close to the track; David's eyes blazed in the reflection. "But someday, Nicole, it will be something."

Regret washed over her. "I never really knew you, David, did I?"

"No, you didn't."

"Yet you always cared for me anyway. Why?"

He almost smiled. "Maybe I am grandiose enough to think I knew you better than you knew you."

"I wish I was as fine a person as you think I am."

He touched her hand that lay on Liz-Bette's head. "But you see, I was right all along. You are."

thirty-four

5 September 1944

Liz-Bette and I are on another transport, packed
into a cattle car with twice as many people as the
train that left Paris. It is twice as hot, twice as
uncomfortable.

David did jump that night. Twenty-seven other
people did, too, including Philippe Kohn and his sister Rose-Marie. M. Kohn, his son Georges-André, and
the rest of his family stayed on the train.

Some hours after the escape, the train ground to
a halt. Three of Brunner's aides burst into the car. We
were marched into a field to be shot in reprisal for
the escape. The SS threw shovels and ordered us to
dig our own graves. But then an officer of the
German Air Force intervened and said that the only
people who were going to be shot were the SS men
who allowed the Jews to escape. He put us back on
the train and we began rolling again.

Liz-Bette and I were transferred soon afterward to

another train that deposited us in Westerbork, in Holland. Why? Who knows? We stayed there approximately a week. Practically no one spoke French. Then, they put us on a massive transport that left on 3 September.

We have been traveling for three days and two nights. There are no seats, no space, no quiet. We have one overflowing toilet bucket that gets emptied through a crack in the floor.

I heard a couple making love in the dark last night. I didn't want to hear, but I heard.

Where are we going? Where are the Allies? Even if they do not come, why don't they bomb the rail lines?

"Nicole, is there water?" Liz-Bette asked.

"They haven't given us any today. Try to sleep, Liz-Bette. The time will pass faster. Maybe when you wake up we will be there. You will go straight to the infirmary. You'll have soup and medicine. You will get well."

Liz-Bette closed her eyes, and Nicole put her head in her hands. She was so lonely. No one else on the car but Liz-Bette spoke French. A cramp gripped her. She had fought the urge to use the bucket for hours.

But she had no alternative, so she began to wend her way through the packed car, murmuring "Excuse me, please," hopeful that she could be understood.

Finally, she reached the bucket. A tall man leered at her. How could she possibly use it in front of him? "Could you look away, please?" she asked in French. He kept leering. A girl sitting nearby scolded him in Dutch, and the man turned to the wall.

Nicole nodded her thanks. *"Spreekt U Nederlands?"* the girl asked. When Nicole didn't respond, she switched to French. "You were speaking French just now. Is this better?"

"Yes." The oddest feeling came over Nicole, as if she knew this girl. She was about Nicole's age, perhaps a little younger. Petite, thin, and pale, with dark, thoughtful eyes. She carried a coat over her arm.

"You are staring at me," the girl pointed out.

"Sorry."

"You're still doing it. Just an observation."

Another cramp hit Nicole. "Excuse me, but I need to use the—"

"It's all right," the girl assured her, holding her coat open for Nicole. "This will give you some privacy."

"Thank you." Nicole squatted over the bucket.

"All I ask is that you do the same for me when the time comes."

"Yes, I will." Nicole finished as quickly as possible, then wiped her palms on her skirt. It was the best she could do. Nicole stared at the girl again—something about her was right on the edge of Nicole's memory.

"You are doing it again," the girl noted, as an old man

roughly pushed between them. They moved as far as possible from the bucket, stepping over sleeping bodies. "At least it doesn't smell quite as bad over here."

"I know this will sound insane," Nicole began slowly, "but I feel as if I know you."

"Have you ever been to Amsterdam?"

Nicole shook her head. "I'm from Paris."

"Well, I've never been there. Although I will go someday, I can assure you of that."

Something long buried in Nicole's mind swam upward until, like an air bubble in a pond, it surfaced. "I do know you," Nicole declared. "Your name is . . . Anne Frank."

The girl looked incredulous. "That's right. Who are you?"

"Nicole Bernhardt." Waves of knowledge washed over her. "I know so much about you! You were in hiding for a long time—in a place you called the Secret Annex."

"How could you know that?"

"You were with your parents, and your older sister . . . Margot! And other people—"

"M. Pfeffer and the Van Pels, they're all back there asleep—"

"No! Van Daans!" Nicole exclaimed.

"This is impossible, Nicole. I only called them by that name in my writing. How could you possibly know that?"

"And Peter! Your boyfriend's name is Peter!"

"How could you know that?"

A sudden bump on the track jostled them; they reached to steady each other—Nicole felt as if jolts of electricity were coursing through her. "I remember . . . you thought your parents disapproved that you were kissing him."

Anne's voice became a whisper. "How is this possible?"

"I don't know—" Nicole began, then stopped. Because suddenly, she did know. "You kept a diary. I read it."

"But I left my diary in the Annex when the Gestapo came. You couldn't have read it."

"I did, though."

"How?"

"I don't know," Nicole admitted. "Believe me, I wish I did."

Anne gave her an arched look. "This is a very strange conversation."

The train lurched violently. People cried out in fear, but Nicole was oblivious as a new thought surfaced, one so absurd that she was almost too embarrassed to say it. "Anne, I feel like it was—I know this will sound crazy—but I feel like it was in the future."

"This is a joke, right? Peter put you up to this."

"No."

"Daddy, then, to take my mind off—"

"No."

Anne looked dubious. "Maybe you are a mind reader." She closed her eyes, fingertips on her temples. "What number am I thinking of right now?"

"I have no idea," Nicole admitted. "Anne, do you believe in time travel?"

"Science fiction? Like Jules Verne? I'm to believe you're

from the future? Really, I'm much more intelligent than I look." She wagged a finger at Nicole. "I know someone put you up to this—"

"Nicole? Where is my sister? I lost my sister! Nicole?" Liz-Bette was screaming, pushing blindly through the car.

"Here! Liz-Bette, I'm here!" Nicole waved her arms high so that her sister could see, and Liz-Bette edged through to her.

"I woke up and couldn't find you," she sobbed, clutching Nicole. Her words were interrupted by deep, hacking coughs. "I was so scared. I thought they had taken you away."

"Never. I'll never leave you. Lie down and go back to sleep, Liz-Bette. I'll stay right by you."

"Here?"

"Here." She and Anne moved a bit so that Liz-Bette could stretch out.

"Your sister?" Anne asked softly.

Nicole nodded.

"And the rest of your family is here?"

"No. My mother was on another transport. They shot my father."

"I'm so sorry."

"And my boyfriend. My best friend, too, I'm sure." Nicole's blood ran cold with bitterness. "Anne? Do you think God is watching us right now?"

"Yes."

"Someone told me God must be on vacation. Maybe

there is no God. Maybe we just made Him up so we wouldn't all go crazy."

Anne's gaze was steady. "I don't believe that."

"Then nothing makes any sense. My best friend died because she tried to save our lives. My boyfriend died because he felt betrayed by my father, so he betrayed us in return. My father died to save Jewish lives, but ended up killing innocent people. All that suffering and death. I can't make any sense of it. So I really want to know, where is God now?"

"Right here," Anne said softly. "Right beside us."

"We're in a cattle car!"

Anne lifted her chin toward the barred window at the top of the car. "But we can still see the stars."

Nicole looked out at the sliver of sky. "Anne, are you scared?"

"Yes."

"Even though you have faith in God?"

"Yes." Nicole heard the tremor in Anne's voice as the train slowed. "Nicole, I want to ask you something. If you really are from the future, and you read my diary, then you must know what happens to me."

"No—"

"You can tell me," Anne insisted. "Please."

Nicole hesitated. "I never finished it."

"You never . . . ?" Anne burst out laughing. "Very funny. Now I know that Peter put you up to this!"

"I did read a very juicy part about you and him, though, about how you loved him and didn't think you needed to wait until you were a 'suitable age.'"

Anne grinned mischievously. "I am a free thinker."

"You sound like my sister. She's planning to run away with Clark Gable."

Anne leaned close, a conspiratorial gleam in her eye. "Don't tell Peter, but I don't think he's the perfect boy for me after all. I'd like to break a million hearts, wouldn't you?"

"Oh, yes."

"And see the whole world—"

"And have a million adventures."

"I want to see Paris."

"It's wonderful! After the war I'll take you everywhere," Nicole promised. "The Louvre, the Eiffel Tower—"

"Where do you want to go?"

Nicole thought a moment. "Palestine, maybe."

"Palestine? Really?"

"I think a friend of mine is there."

"Then you'll go there." Anne squeezed Nicole's hand. "Everything is possible. Don't you see?"

Anne's eyes searched Nicole's, and Nicole saw herself reflected in them—grimy, hungry, lice-ridden. But this much she knew: She would not change places for a moment with the people who had made her that way.

"Yes, Anne," Nicole whispered. "Yes. I do."

thirty-five

A squeal of brakes, a long grinding, as the train slowed, then stopped. "Have we arrived?" Liz-Bette asked hoarsely. "Can we get water?"

People shouted as families tried to organize themselves and their belongings. From outside came the sound of amplified German. The car's door swung open, and uniformed SS—also some men in blue-and-white striped prison garb—rushed in, shouting orders. *"Dalli, dalli, dalli, alles hinaus!"* the SS men bellowed, swinging their truncheons. *"Schneller, schneller!"* At the same time, the men in the striped uniforms were shouting in different languages. It was bedlam.

"French, we are French, I don't understand, what do we do?" Nicole cried, holding tightly to Liz-Bette's hand.

"Go!" one of the uniformed prisoners instructed them, in Polish-accented French. "Leave your luggage, you'll get it later. Go, go, go!"

"We have no luggage. Where are we?"

"Birkenau! Go! Go, be healthy!"

"What does he mean, Nicole?"" Liz-Bette asked.

"I don't know."

"*Schnell, Juden, Schnell!*" More orders were broadcast by loudspeaker. "*Alles austreten, alle Bagage hinlegen. Alles austreten, alle Bagage hinlegen.*"

Nicole and Liz-Bette stepped out of the car and into the night. Up and down the track, hundreds of other frightened people climbed out of cattle cars, the chaotic scene illuminated by two huge beacons. Nicole scanned the crowd for Anne, but couldn't find her.

That was when the horrible smell hit. Cloying, nauseating; the odor of a stomach-turning barbecue. "What is that smell?" Liz-Bette gagged.

"I don't know."

"Jews!" Another prisoner shouted in French. "Those of you who can walk, move on. Those too sick to walk, trucks will take you where you need to be."

"Can we wait for the truck, Nicole?" Liz-Bette begged. "I am so tired."

"Yes," Nicole agreed, since Liz-Bette could barely hold herself up. "We'll wait here and—"

"No!" The French-speaking prisoner insisted. "No truck! You must walk, be healthy! *Walk.*" Something told Nicole to follow his directions, so she pulled her sister along. Looking back, she saw a few dozen exhausted old people sitting on the platform.

As the crowd pressed forward, the intense smell grew worse. It seemed to come from a building several hundred yards away that belched thick smoke from its smokestack.

"Men left, women right, men left, women right, men left, women right!" the SS men roared, their words translated by other prisoners. "Separate and keep walking! Form fives, form fives!"

Many families were trying to proceed as a unit. Directly in front of them, an SS man tore an infant from a woman's arms and flung him toward a group of men. Then, he slammed the woman in the stomach with his truncheon; she collapsed.

Liz-Bette began to cry. "Don't look," Nicole said sharply. "Act as if it is something you are reading in a book, not real. Don't look."

Moments later, two long columns of several hundred people, separated by sex, stood on the platform. Nicole and Liz-Bette were at the outside edge of the women's group, closest to the road. Across that road was a fence topped by barbed wire; beyond that, a mass of low-slung buildings. What had the man called this place? Birkenau? Across the fence, more prisoners watched those arriving. In the harsh light, Nicole could see that they were ghastly thin.

"Hey, Vel d'Hiv girl! Hey!"

Someone was yelling in French from the other side of the fence. Nicole's eyes searched the faceless forms, perhaps forty yards distant, trying to discern who was calling. "Hey, Vel d'Hiv girl! Over here!"

There! A prisoner—impossible to see how old she was or what she looked like—was waving her arms. "Vel d'Hiv girl!"

Nicole waved back. "Me? You mean me?"

"Yes, you! I know you! Listen to me. Be healthy!"

"Who is that?" Liz-Bette asked dully.

Nicole squinted. "I don't know."

"Vel d'Hiv girl, I know you!"

"Who are you?" Nicole yelled.

"I am Paulette. From the Vel. I helped your friend escape. 'Water for the children!' "

Nicole tried to recall—it was so long ago—more than two years. Had she met someone at the Vel named Paulette? She searched her memory. There was Claire, of course. The mother with the baby who had stood behind Nicole in line for the toilet. And a beautiful girl with flaxen hair who had helped—

Nicole gasped. Was this her? "You had golden hair?" Nicole called.

"Yes, Vel d'Hiv girl! You must listen. Go to the right! Go to the right! Always go to the right!"

Liz-Bette looked up at Nicole. "Did she lose her mind? Is that why she is yelling?"

"I know her." Nicole cupped her hands to her mouth to call back. "What do you mean, to the right?" But the din on the platform escalated, as the SS waded into several family groups that were refusing to separate, swinging their truncheons. The girl shook her head that she couldn't hear Nicole.

The column of women moved forward. Nicole had no

choice but to move with it. When she looked across the barbed-wire fence again, Paulette was gone.

~

Their column clomped along. Escape was impossible. Not only were they weak with hunger, but ranks of heavily armed SS guarded them, weapons at the ready.

"What's happening?" Liz-Bette asked. "Where are we going?"

"I think we're being admitted to a camp. Hold my hand. Don't let go." As the ranks pressed forward, Nicole could see a uniformed Nazi at the end of the platform, a shorter SS man by his side, bullwhip in hand. As each woman approached, the taller man would make a quick appraisal, point right or left with his chin; the SS man indicated the direction with his whip.

Nicole watched carefully. An elderly woman was sent to the left, then a girl younger than Liz-Bette. A woman who looked to be in her thirties was sent to right. Suddenly, Liz-Bette pointed. "Look, Nicole, it's your friend from the train."

Up ahead, Anne and a girl who looked like her—her sister?—approached the two Germans. They were sent to the right. Nicole leaned toward Liz-Bette. "Liz-Bette, listen to me. No matter what happens, we must go to the right. Do you understand?"

"Why?"

"Just do it!"

The column pressed forward. Nicole was four rows away from the end of the platform. Right, left, left, left, left, right, left, left, right, left.

Nicole was next. She stepped forward and stood before the Nazis, grasping Liz-Bette's hand until the last instant. The taller one regarded her. Time stopped. Right, his chin jerked.

"Nicole?" Liz-Bette called anxiously.

"I'll be right here," Nicole called, backing toward the right. "I swear it. I can still see you. As long as I can see you, we are still together." Liz-Bette stood before the Nazi's diffident scrutiny.

Please, Nicole prayed. Dear God, please.

Liz-Bette coughed, a deep, hacking cough. The Nazi's chin jerked left.

"No!" Nicole screamed. *"Nein!"*

"Let her go," a prisoner in a striped uniform told Nicole. "She's bound for the ovens. Save your own skin." But Nicole ran back to the tall man who had made the selection.

"Please," she begged in French, pointing at Liz-Bette. "She can come to the right with me. She can!" He did not look at her. So she turned to the shorter SS man. "Please. Let her come to me. Or let me be with my sister."

He chuckled and pointed to the left with his bullwhip. *"Du? Lentz?"*

"Lentz," Nicole echoed, nodding furiously. *"Ja. Lentz."*

"Jawohl, Lentz, Jude!" the SS man mock-saluted her. *"Jawohl, Jude, Heil Hitler!"* He pointed left again as all

around him on the platform his fellow Germans laughed uproariously. Nicole ran to Liz-Bette and hugged her.

"You didn't leave me."

"No. Didn't I promise?"

The two columns were now separated by a rank of SS— Nicole saw Anne in the other column, not twenty feet away. A woman had her arms around Anne's older sister, who was sobbing. Anne stood alone.

"Anne?" Nicole called. "Anne!"

Anne turned. "Nicole?" Her eyes seemed to overwhelm her pale face. "Nicole, I'm scared. I am so scared." Nicole wished that she could offer Anne the same strength that Anne had offered her on the train. But she didn't have Anne's faith; she wasn't strong enough or brave enough to—

"Anne?"

"Yes, Nicole?"

"Anne, listen to me. It's important!" One of the SS men glared at her, but she didn't care. "I lied before. I do know what happens to you!"

"You do?" Anne's eyes grew wide.

"Yes," Nicole insisted. "You become a famous writer. And you break a million hearts."

Anne wrapped her arms around herself, as though they were Nicole's arms. "Thank you," she said simply. That was when Nicole and Liz-Bette's column began to move forward.

༄

It seemed the only word on the planet was *Schnell.*

"*Schnell, Schnell!*" the SS ordered, swinging their truncheons to make the women run.

"I'm too tired to run," Liz-Bette panted.

"You can do it," Nicole coaxed.

"*Schnell, Juden, Schnell!*" The women ran through a gate toward the building with the big smokestack. The vile smell was overpowering. The ground sloped downward and an entrance to its interior opened before them. With more shouts, the SS forced the women into an underground room.

Nicole held fast to Liz-Bette as prisoners in uniform shouted directions to them. "You will have a shower and be deloused! Leave your clothes in a pile for later!"

Everyone is either shot or marched into a big room—for a shower, they'll tell you—

Nicole felt weak. She looked around—the walls were covered with signs, most making reference to LAUS. She knew enough German to understand that was the word for lice.

It was a delousing procedure. David was wrong. She was sure of it.

"It is a shower," she told Liz-Bette firmly. "Disinfecting. It will take away your itching. That will be wonderful."

"Hurry, hurry!" the uniformed prisoners shouted. "Into the shower room. Take off everything!" Nicole and Liz-Bette stripped naked as the girls and women around them did the same. Most used their hands to try to cover themselves.

Liz-Bette crossed her arms over

"I'm embarrassed, Nicole," she whimp

"Pretend you have on a beautiful b

Nicole told her. "The blue one that matche

"Into the shower! Hurry, hurry!"

"Your gown is very lovely, but it could use a

ing." She took Liz-Bette's hand as they were herde

a doorway into the shower room, and looked aroun

eyes adjusted to the murky light. Showerheads. Yes. A d

No, fourteen. Spaced out on the walls. She went limp w

relief. "You see the spigots, Liz-Bette? It is going to be grand

to be clean."

More people were pressed into the room. It was getting
dangerously crowded. How could all these people be
deloused at the same time? The crush forced them toward
the rear wall. There were panicked shouts as naked men
were pushed into the room. The heavy door clanged shut.

"I want my maman!" Liz-Bette howled. "I want my
maman!"

"Stop it, stop it, stop it!" Nicole screamed. She clapped her
hands over her ears and squeezed her eyes shut. It was too
much to ask—she could not be strong. She wanted to lose her
mind, tear her hair out, to beg someone, anyone, for her life.

"I'm sorry, Nicole," Liz-Bette said. "I'm sorry that I was
sick. You should have gone with Anne."

It had come to this: Her twelve-year-old sister blamed
herself instead of the ones who were guilty. That, Nicole

ld not allow her to do. She met her sister's panicky gaze
h steady eyes.

"Listen to me, Liz-Bette," Nicole said, bending close to her
ister's ear. "You are not responsible. *They* are responsible. I
am here because I chose to be. Do you hear me?"

Liz-Bette nodded.

"I will give you Papa's Shabbos blessing. It will be my
voice and my heart, but his, too. And others, everyone who
ever loved you. Do you understand?"

Liz-Bette nodded again. Something like marbles clattered
through the ceiling and fell to the floor. People howled in
fear, pushing wildly, coughing. Nicole gently placed her hands
on her sister's head. "*Yiverechecha Adonai viyismerecha,*"
Nicole prayed. "May God bless you and keep you. *Yaer Adonai
panav elecha viyichunecha.* May God's countenance shine
upon you and illuminate you. *Esai Adonai panav elecha
vasham lecha shalom.* May God turn His countenance to you
and bring you peace."

People shrieked and tore at their throats, choking. Nicole
and Liz-Bette began to choke, too. But Nicole forced herself
to keep talking to her sister. "God is watching us, Liz-Bette.
*Shema Yisroel, Adonai Elohenu, Adonai Echad; Shema
Yisroel—*"

In the tiniest voice, Liz-Bette joined her. "*Adonai Elohenu,
Adonai Echad.*"

Now, bodies were falling to the floor. "*Shema Yisroel,
Adonai Elohenu, Adonai Echad.* Hear O Israel, the Lord is

Our God, the Lord is One. *Shema Yisroel, Adonai Elohenu, Adonai Echad."*

"Shema Yisroel, Adonai Elohenu . . ."

"I love you, Liz-Bette," Nicole whispered.

Then, there was only silence.

thirty-six

The blaring high-pitched whine of sirens. A terrible pounding inside her head. Raw, rhythmic waves of pain. Nicole clamped her hands over her eyes and moaned. It was as if her mind were swimming through muck, coming up from another place. Who she was and where she was, and what had happened, returned to her slowly, like faces materializing on a developing photograph.

"Nicole? Nicole?" Someone was calling to her from very far away. "Nicole? Nicole?"

The voice came closer, far too loud, reverberating like exploding bombs, punctuated by an insistent *whup-whup, whup-whup.*

"Nicole, can you hear me?" *Whup-whup, whup-whup.*

"I hear you," Nicole mumbled through parched lips. She recognized that voice, didn't she? Yes, she did. Ms. Zooms, her English teacher.

"Nicole?" Ms. Zooms repeated. "I couldn't understand you. What did you say?"

Nicole licked her lips and forced her mouth to form distinct words. "Stop. Calling. My. Name." She tried to get her bearings. She was lying on her back. On something hard. "Am I alive?"

"Yes. Very much alive." Ms. Zooms' normally bombastic voice was surprisingly soothing.

Whup-whup, whup-whup. What was that noise?

"What's her name? Can she open her eyes?"

"Can you open your eyes, Nicole?" Ms. Zooms asked. "There's a paramedic here."

Nicole shook her head, which sent waves of pain coursing through her body.

"Too much sensory input, too fast," she heard the paramedic explain. "It's not uncommon after something like this."

What was he talking about? What had happened? A breeze tickled Nicole's face. She smelled burning leaves.

I must be outside. But how did I get out here?

"Where am I?" Nicole managed.

"Outside the state museum," the paramedic replied. "Your vitals are fine. We called your mom, and she's meeting you at Memorial."

"Memorial what?"

"Memorial Hospital. The doctors need to check you out. Think you could open those peepers now, nice and slow?"

Her eyelids felt leaden. She covered them with her hand, then forced them open, squinting between her fingers into the too-bright morning sun. Her view was partly blocked by a red-haired man with a stethoscope around his neck.

"Welcome back, Nicole. I'm Sam. How many fingers do you see?" He held up two.

"More than one, less than three."

He grinned and turned to Ms. Zooms. "Other than having the mother of all headaches for a while, it looks like she'll live. We'll take her to Memorial just to be on the safe side. Don't let her move around too much."

"I'll see to that, thank you," Ms. Zooms agreed, as Sam hurried toward a man with a walkie-talkie. Nicole craned her neck carefully, looking around.

She was on a bench in the plaza. There were scores of police, heavily armed SWAT teams running to and fro, and many ambulances. Overhead, she counted two—no, three—helicopters. That accounted for the annoying *whup-whup*s. But what was happening? She felt off-kilter, caught in someone else's skin. Suddenly, something essential deep inside of her shifted, an earthquake of the self, pieces falling not out of place but rather into it. And she remembered.

The state museum. An exhibition about Anne Frank. Doom with a gun. Gunshots. Terror. Panic. Bodies crushing bodies. Bodies falling. Mimi. Oh, God, Mimi—

"Nico!"

Suddenly, Mimi was flying toward her. Nicole hugged her. "I had to wait forever for the paramedics to tell me I'm fine, which I could have told them but no one would listen to me," Mimi reported. "Are you okay?"

"Miss Baker, good to see you in one piece," Ms. Zooms

242

said. "Can I count on you to stay here with Miss Burns until the paramedic comes back?"

"Absolutely."

"If Miss Burns' condition changes, scream." Ms. Zooms gave Mimi one last look for emphasis, then hustled off.

"What happened, Mimi? The last thing I remember, we were in a crush trying to get out—"

"I hyperventilated and we fell into this mosh pit. You got slammed into the door—*bam!* You were out cold. God, it was scary. I managed to drag you out of there."

"Thanks."

"Anytime."

Whup-whup. Nicole looked up. Another helicopter, this one bearing the logo of an all-news cable network, joined the three in the skies above them.

"It's like we're in a movie," Mimi said.

"Only we're not. It's real." Nicole's head pounded. "How many people did Doom get?"

"I don't know."

"Did they catch him?"

Mimi cocked her chin toward a paddy wagon surrounded by a sea of blue uniforms. "In there."

"How does a person get that twisted?" Nicole wondered.

Mimi shrugged. "Who knows. How's your head?"

"I plan to live."

Mimi looked at her quizzically. "Odd thing to say, but good to know."

Sam the paramedic loped back over to them. "Hey, how ya doing, Nicole? Double vision? Vomiting? Fainting?"

"None of the above."

"Great. We're kinda shorthanded. Think we can get you into an ambulance under your own steam?"

"Sure." Sam and Mimi helped Nicole up. For a moment she felt dizzy, but it passed. They guided her toward an ambulance as Mr. Urkin's amplified voice reverberated through the air.

"All West students not receiving medical attention are to line up by class in front of the Assembly building for a head count. Immediately."

"That means me," Mimi said. "I'll come to the hospital as soon as they let me."

Nicole hugged her again. "I'm so glad you're okay."

"Right back at'cha." Mimi headed for the Assembly building. Nicole saw Suzanne catch up with her, Jack at her side.

It came back to her like a sucker punch to the gut. Jack. The bus ride. He'd saved her a seat. Put his arm around her.

It's about Suzanne. I'm crazy about her.

"Hey, you're looking a little green around the gills all of a sudden," Sam said. "You okay?"

No. Nothing was okay. She nodded anyway, and he helped her into the ambulance.

ॐ

"Mom, I'm fine," Nicole insisted. "Can't we just go home?"

"Soon, sweetie." She trotted along as a hospital orderly

rolled Nicole into an antiseptic-looking room at Memorial Hospital. "It's just for observation."

"Did you hear any news while you were waiting in the ER? Did anyone die?"

"I don't know. Everyone was saying it was that Hayden boy. How did he just slip through the system?"

"You need help getting into the bed?" the orderly asked Nicole.

"No, thanks. I don't even need to be here." Nicole climbed off the gurney and got onto the bed. She eyed the TV bolted to the wall. "I've got to know what's going on. Can we turn it on?"

The orderly shook his head. "Not without a requisition."

"Who do I have to see to do that?" Mrs. Burns asked.

"Accounting." He hesitated. "I'm not supposed to do this, but . . ." He went to the TV, punched a code into the cable box, and clicked on the power.

"Thanks." Nicole's eyes were already glued to the screen as he wheeled the gurney out of the room. An aerial view of the state capital government plaza, still a mass of emergency vehicles, filled the screen, with the word LIVE superimposed on it.

"Recapping our top story," said the news announcer. "At a traveling exhibit called *Anne Frank in the World*, gunfire evidently erupted while the state museum was filled with high school students. It has been confirmed that some students have been taken by ambulance to local hospitals. A male juvenile is reportedly being held by police as the suspect."

245

The newscaster narrated as taped footage was shown. It was surreal. Nicole saw people she knew outside the museum, hugging and crying. At any moment, she expected to see the aerial camera zooming in on herself.

"We have a new development," the anchorwoman cut in. "We're going live to a press conference being held by Chief of Police Shanika Brown, and the head of security for the *Anne Frank in the World* exhibition, Moshe Ben-Ami."

The cameras cut to the steps of the museum. A crowd of reporters shouted questions.

"Chief Brown, how many dead?"

"Was this an anti-Semitic hate crime?"

"Any truth that foreign terrorists might be involved?"

Chief Brown, a petite African American woman, stepped to the mike. "I have a brief prepared statement." She waited for the crowd to quiet, then began to read from a note card. "Today, students at the state museum were the victims of a cruel and dangerous prank. No weapons were involved, and fortunately, no one died."

"What?" Nicole yelped. "There were shots, I heard them!"

"This morning, at approximately nine-forty-five, three students from East High School threw lit firecrackers at students from West High School. In the resulting panic, two dozen students were injured. Fifteen were treated and released at the scene, eight are hospitalized in satisfactory condition, and one student is still in surgery with a compound fracture to his right leg. Police have released a student who had been detained on suspicion of having used a weapon. I give you now Moshe Ben-Ami, chief of security for the exhibition."

"It wasn't Doom," Nicole said, dazed. "We were all so sure."

On TV, a burly man stepped to the microphone. "I am Moshe Ben-Ami," he said with a slight accent. "First let me assure you that our excellent security precluded a gun from ever entering the museum. Moreover, the entire exhibition is under video surveillance, so we were able to review the tapes and quickly identify the perpetrators. Chief Brown has informed me that they are now under arrest. Thank you."

Chief Brown came forward to take the barrage of questions that followed. "Amazing." Mrs. Burns clicked off the TV. "You should rest now, sweetie."

Nicole slumped back against her pillows. One thought kept playing in her mind: Doom hadn't done anything wrong at all.

thirty-seven

"Nicole? Nicole?"

Nicole opened her eyes. Little Bit stood by her bedside, looking down at her. "Why are people always calling my name?" Nicole said groggily. "What time is it?"

"Eight. Are you okay?"

"You woke me to ask if I'm okay?"

"Mom said we need to keep an eye on you in case your brain got damaged yesterday, though personally I don't think it was in such great shape before."

"I'm going back to sleep." She rolled over and snuggled into the pillow.

"Want to know what I heard on the news just now?"

"No."

"They released the boy with the broken leg from the hospital," Little Bit reported. "Want to know what else?"

Nicole groaned.

"They're playing the football game. The mayor said it's important to show the world our town's spirit and it's not fair to punish everyone for what just a few kids did."

" 'This is Little Bit Burns, signing off,' " Nicole concluded for her sister.

"It's Elizabeth."

"Lemme sleep." Nicole pulled the blanket up to her chin and nuzzled into her pillow again. But sleep would not come. She kept seeing images from the day before in her mind: the crush of bodies, the panic, the chaos. She opened her eyes. Little Bit was at her dresser, trying on one of her bracelets. "What do you think you're doing?"

"Nothing." Red-faced, Little Bit took it off quickly.

"How many times have I told you not to touch my stuff?"

"Hey, you two." Mrs. Burns walked in, dressed for work. "How are you feeling, sweetie?"

"Ready to become an only child," Nicole replied.

Her mom smiled. "Feeling fine, then? No dizziness, headache, nausea?"

Nicole sat up. "I'm fine, Mom. Really."

"Good. Because you've got a visitor for breakfast."

Mimi appeared in the doorway, a loaded breakfast tray in her hands. "*Excusez-moi,* but is Sarah Bernhardt hungry?" She set the tray on Nicole's nightstand.

"Who's Sarah Bernhardt?" Little Bit asked.

"She was a French actress," Mrs. Burns began, "who was famous for being so—"

"Dramatic," Nicole finished. "A theater in Paris was named after her, but the Nazis changed its name during the war because she was Jewish."

"What war?" Little Bit asked.

"World War Two," Mrs. Burns replied, regarding her eldest quizzically. "How did you know that, sweetie?"

Nicole shrugged.

"Maybe by mistake she actually listened in French class one day," Little Bit theorized. "Mom, can you give me and Britnee a ride to the game this afternoon?"

"I'm showing a house. But come downstairs and we'll discuss it with your father." Mrs. Burns' cell phone rang just as she ushered Little Bit out of the room.

Mimi sat on Nicole's bed and pulled her legs into a lotus position. "So, Nico, how are you feeling? Really."

"Decent." Nicole pulled a pillow onto her lap. "Yesterday feels like some parallel universe, though. I can't get over that Doom didn't do anything."

"Me, neither." Mimi reached for an orange section on Nicole's breakfast tray and popped it into her mouth. "We all just assumed—"

"That was so messed up, Meem. We should apologize to him."

"Yeah. If he'll even speak to us. So, are you up for telling me about Jack?"

∽

When Nicole finished explaining what had happened on the bus, Mimi just sat there, staring into space.

"I say we put me up against the wall and shoot me," Mimi finally said.

"Because—"

"It's my fault. I was so sure he was into you."

"It's okay, Meem. Jack isn't important."

"Excuse me. Did Girl X just say *I isn't important?*"

"Weird, I know." Nicole searched for the hurt she'd felt when Jack had told her he was crazy about Suzanne. But it was like wiggling her tongue in the hole where her wisdom tooth had been before it had been pulled. She knew she'd been in the worst pain, but now that it was gone, it was hard to remember.

"So, does Jack know how you felt about him?" Mimi asked.

"Not unless you told him. And you didn't."

Mimi cringed. "Well, at the museum yesterday I might have said something vacuous like, 'You and Nicole make a cute couple.' "

Nicole groaned.

"I'm sorry, Nico." Mimi twisted a finger into the love beads she wore. "Okay, there is only one viable course of action."

Nicole gave her a dubious look. "Which is?"

"We go to the football game," Mimi decreed. "You see Jack, Jack sees you, you act like he's just some guy, no biggie. Fade to black. It's the sure path to damage control. Trust me."

"I hate it when you say 'trust me,' Meem. I really do."

～

The sun shone brightly, the temperature hung in the low sixties, and the streets leading to the stadium were clogged with cars. The annual East-West football game drew thousands of spectators. Nicole and Mimi walked uphill toward the stadium amidst the high-spirited crowd. "Doesn't this seem weird, Meem, after what happened yesterday?"

"I find life in general to be weird, but you know how skewed I am . . . in a charming sort of way." She scrutinized her friend. "You got that sweater in middle school, I remember when we bought it. I thought you threw it out."

"I guess I didn't." When Nicole had opened her closet to get dressed for the game, she'd had the strangest feeling of being overwhelmed. There were so many clothes—items she'd worn only once, some she'd never worn at all. Expensive outfits hung half-on and half-off hangers, while others were in a wrinkled heap on the floor entangled with dozens of shoes. She'd pulled on the sturdiest things she saw—the sweater and a pair of jeans.

At the crest of the hill they joined the line to enter the stadium. "Got your ID card?" Mimi asked, as the West drum corps started their military cadence. *Rat-a-tat-tat-rat-a-tat-tat.*

A jolt of anxiety shot up Nicole's neck. "Why? What if I don't have it?"

"Then you don't get in the game for free. You know that." Mimi peered at her. "Are you sure you're okay?"

"I'm fine."

The long line wended its way to the entrance of the stadium, splitting in two at the gate. "Students, have your ID cards ready," a bored policeman repeated. "West students to the right, all others to the left!"

The line edged forward, but Nicole didn't budge. "Yo, babe, move it!" a guy down the line catcalled.

"Move this!" Mimi shouted back at him, then turned to Nicole. "We can leave if you don't feel good."

"It's . . . nothing. Free-floating anxiety," Nicole added with a self-conscious laugh, forcing her feet forward. Mimi flashed her ID card at the guard monitoring the entrance. Nicole's heart pounded as she flashed her card, too. It was so bizarre. Was this some weird aftereffect of her concussion?

As they made their way through the bleachers looking for seats, she felt a little better. West's marching band struck up the school fight song. Instantly, the crowd was on its feet waving blue and white pom-poms and singing lustily with the band. In retaliation, the East band started its fight song. The musical mayhem made Nicole dizzy. Mimi didn't notice; she was scoping out the crowd for Jack.

"There he is." Mimi subtly cocked her head. "Twenty yard line, about twenty rows up from the field. Don't look like you're looking."

"I'm not," Nicole said, her head clearing. "Let's just go sit down."

They made their way past knees toward two empty seats. "Mobile ptomaine, a.k.a. Chrissy, just joined Jack and Eddie," Mimi reported. "Uh, Suzanne is sitting next to him. Don't—"

Nicole looked. And shrugged.

Mimi regarded her. "Does my face by any chance read, 'Deeply concerned for best friend's mental health'?"

"What do you want me to say, Meem? That I wish Jack was with me instead of with Suzanne? I do. But wishing won't change anything, so I might as well accept it. How's that?"

"Frighteningly mature."

The crowd roared as the West Bears ran onto the field, and the band tore into Sousa's "The Thunderer." It was deafening. Nicole tried to swallow but felt like her throat was clamping up. It was awful. If she could just swallow, then maybe—

She jumped up. "I've got to get a drink."

Mimi stood, too. "I'll come with—"

Nicole was already pushing past all those knees and heading for the water fountain at the top of the concrete steps. It was only as she waited in line for a drink that Mimi caught up with her. "What's up with you, Nico? Are you sick?"

It was Nicole's turn at the fountain. She guzzled as if she hadn't had a drink in days, months, years. "Leave some for the fish," the next guy in line cracked.

Mimi yanked Nicole's arm. "Okay, you are acting truly strange. I'm calling your mom."

"No. I'm okay," Nicole insisted, and she did feel better.

Just then, the old town air-raid siren sounded to signal the end of the pregame pageantry. "Attention, please! Ladies and gentlemen!" A voice boomed over the public address system. "Please rise to honor America and join in the singing of 'The Star-Spangled Banner'!"

Nicole stood very still. She heard another amplified voice, making another announcement. In French.

Attention, attention! Dans le cas d'une mort subite, apportez le corps du mort vers la section deux cent au premier niveau du stade.

Nicole froze.

"Nico?" Mimi called. "Okay, you are officially weirding me out now."

Mimi's voice seemed so far away. But the announcement over the loudspeaker was inescapable.

Attention, attention! Dans le cas d'une mort subite, apportez le corps du mort vers la section deux cent au premier niveau du stade.

"In the event of an unexpected death, bring the body to area two hundred on the main level," Nicole whispered.

"You're scaring the hell out of me, Nico." Mimi guided her to the outer fence of the stadium. "Stay right here. Don't move. I'm getting help. I swear, I'll be right back."

In the event of an unexpected death, bring the body to area two hundred on the main level.

Nicole huddled against the fence. She was there, and at the same time, not there. She was someplace else. It came to her, like flashes from some long-forgotten dream:

Paris. The Occupation. The Vel d'Hiv roundup. The black

market. The attic. Drancy. The transports. The selection. The gas chamber.

"O'er the land of the free, and the home of the brave!"

The crowd cheered as the national anthem ended; Nicole barely heard it. As West kicked off to East, and its players ran down the field, Nicole ran, too—all the way out of the stadium.

thirty-eight

Nicole stood under a canopy of autumn-hued leaves only blocks from the football stadium, staring at a tidy white frame house with drawn shades. Everyone knew who lived there. But no one she knew had ever been inside.

She rang the bell beside the front door. No answer. She rang again, more insistently this time. Finally, the door opened. With a book in her hand and reading glasses dangling from her neck, there stood Ms. Zooms.

"Miss Burns," the teacher said. "Good to see you hale and hearty, though I can't say I expected you at my front door. Perhaps you've heard that even God took a day of rest?"

"I'm sorry for bothering you at home, Ms. Zooms. But just now I was at the football game and I got this weird feeling, you know? No, how could you know. I'm babbling, right? Right. What I'm trying to say is, I remembered. So I had to come find out the truth."

Ms. Zooms looked at her curiously. "Remembered what, Miss Burns?"

"The Holocaust. What happened. I was there."

Her teacher put a bookmark into her book, then opened the door wider. "Come in," she said.

The living room was surprisingly feminine looking, the couch and matching chair covered in shiny floral material, the carpeting pale rose. Ms. Zooms motioned Nicole to the couch, as she took a seat on the chair. "Now, please explain."

"This is going to sound crazy, Ms. Zooms, but I swear it isn't a prank or anything like that. While I was unconscious I remembered I was a French girl. I was born in Paris in 1927. My father was a doctor—"

"And your name was Nicole Bernhardt," her teacher filled in impatiently. "You're smart but you don't like school, and you play the piano."

"I'm not crazy, Ms. Zooms. I know that's from the biography you gave me at the museum. But the thing is, I really was there. My little sister's name was Liz-Bette and my father looked just like Mr. Urkin. And you were my mother."

Ms. Zooms blanched. "Highly doubtful."

"Then why do I remember things that weren't in the biography?"

"Maybe you were paying better attention to our guest speaker than I thought."

"No, I wasn't," Nicole insisted. "So you have to tell me. Nicole Bernhardt actually existed, didn't she? You couldn't have made her up."

"I didn't."

"I knew it!" Nicole jumped to her feet, trembling. "I was—"

"Sit down, Miss Burns."

"But—"

"Sit. And I'll tell you all about Nicole Bernhardt. Excuse me one moment." Ms. Zooms disappeared into the back of her house briefly, then returned with a massive book in her arms. She set it on the coffee table in front of Nicole. *French Children of the Holocaust, A Memorial,* by Serge Klarsfeld. On the cover was a French identification card with the photo of a pretty young girl.

Ms. Zooms opened to the author's preface. "Read the first paragraph, Miss Burns. Aloud."

"The eyes of 2,500 children gaze at us from across the years in these pages. They are among the more than 11,400 children whose lives are chronicled here, inno- cent children who were taken from their homes and put to death in the Nazi camps. Here are the names, addresses, birth dates, and the truth about what happened to all of these children. Their biographies are brief because their lives were brief. On behalf of the few survivors of their families, this book is their collective gravestone."

Nicole looked at her teacher. "I'm in this book?"

Ms. Zooms opened the book at random and turned her head to read the page number. "Page five hundred. Suzanne Berger, a teenager. Born in Paris, deported August 7, 1942. She looks rather like you."

Nicole frowned. "I don't understand. You said—"

Her teacher moved ahead a few hundred pages, passing

pages filled with photographs and brief biographies. "Ah, look. This girl's name is Nicole. Her photo was taken with some other students. That could be you, too. Born June 5, 1927. Deported January 20, 1944."

Faster and faster, Ms. Zooms flipped. "This girl had a sister a few years younger. This one must have loved to dance, she's dressed for a recital. And here are lists of thousands more children who have no photographs."

Nicole slumped down on the couch. "You made your point. You're telling me that Nicole Bernhardt didn't exist."

"On the contrary, I'm telling you she did. Pieces of her are in hundreds, thousands of children recorded here." Ms. Zooms closed the book, her hand resting on the cover. "All murdered."

"It's not the same. I was going to ask you for the other envelope, where you said what happened to me. But I guess it doesn't matter anymore. I'm sorry to have bothered you." She stood; her teacher walked her to the door.

"Something about the experience yesterday touched you so deeply that it felt real to you," Ms. Zooms said to her at the doorstep. "That's a good thing, Nicole. I suggest you embrace it."

෴

Nicole found her father and Mimi in the kitchen, on the verge of calling the police. Neither of them believed her when she told them that she'd been at Ms. Zooms' house. She apologized for worrying them, and promised Mimi she'd call later. Then she went up to her room, where she lay on her bed, trying to fathom the unfathomable.

If Zooms had invented Nicole Bernhardt, why were so many things about Nicole Bernhardt so vivid? How could she, Nicole Burns, know the things she knew? How? Her eyes lit on Anne Frank's diary, which was on her desk. She stood to get it, and blood rushed to her head in a sudden hot burst. She bent over, hands to knees, temples pounding, a fevered freight train rushing headlong into the tunnel of her mind. Things melted away to other things; another time, another place.

"All that suffering and death. I can't make any sense of it. So I really want to know, where is God now?"

"Right here. Right beside us."

"We're in a cattle car!"

"But we can still see the stars."

"Anne, are you scared?"

"Yes."

"Even though you have faith in God?"

"Yes."

"Nicole, I want to ask you something. If you really are from the future, and you read my diary, then you must know what happens to me."

"No—"

"You can tell me. Please."

"I never finished it."

Nicole searched her mind for more. But the train had passed. It felt so true, that she had known Anne Frank, been on a transport with her. But how could it be, when none of it was real?

When she stood again, the world remained intact. She got Anne's diary from her desk. It wasn't very long; she could read the entire thing tonight. She opened to the first page. Whether or not what she thought had happened to Nicole Bernhardt was real, at least she would know everything that had happened to Anne.

She read for hours. When her mother called her for dinner, she said she wasn't hungry. When she finished the actual diary, she read an afterword that explained what had happened to Anne and her family after their arrival at Auschwitz-Birkenau. There was also a lengthy appendix, a report by an independent Dutch commission, proving beyond the shadow of a doubt that the diary was genuine.

She fell asleep with the book in her hands.

I am so scared. Thousands of us are crammed inside some kind of arena. No food, no water; a terrible stench from people relieving themselves in every corner. How did I get here? An old bearded man in a tallis is praying, a woman croons to her sick baby. A beautiful girl with golden hair takes care of her mother. Her name is Paulette. How do I know this? She looks at me and says, I know you.

But she is too far away for me to hear, so how can
she know—
    "Nicole? Where is my sister? I lost my sister!"
    "Here, Liz-Bette. I'm here!" I take her hand.
We're on the platform at a place called Birkenau.
    "Schnell, Juden, Schnell!"
    A skeletal prisoner calls across barbed wire.
"Vel d'Hiv girl! I know you!" It is Paulette.
    "You had golden hair!" I call back.
    "Go to the right!" Paulette cries. "Always go to
the right!"
    "What do you mean, to the right?" Liz-Bette lets
go of my hand. She runs to the left.
    "No, Liz-Bette, no!"
    A plinking. I can't breathe, I can't breathe, I
can't—

Nicole woke up gasping, soaked with perspiration. From
down the hall she heard her parents' television, the laugh-
track from a sitcom. She was completely safe, at home in her
own bed, in the burbs of America, in the twenty-first century.
    But she had been there, too. She had.

"Always go to the right!"

Nicole closed her eyes again. She could still see Paulette,
with her long golden hair. It was so clear in her mind now.

The girl who had tried to save her life at Birkenau had also helped Claire escape from the Vel. Against the darkness of Nicole's eyelids, Paulette's face aged, like a time-lapse photograph, until she became a woman in her seventies standing before a tenth-grade English class.

Of course! Nicole had felt a connection to Paulette when they'd met after Zooms' class. Now she felt giddy, electrified, vindicated. Zooms was wrong. Nicole really had been there, with Paulette. She had to call Mrs. Litzger-Gold immediately; she ran to get the phone directory from her closet.

Litwin, Martin
Litza, Charles
Litzger-Gold, P

She reached for her phone and glimpsed at her clock. It was past midnight, far too late to call. What would she say: "Sorry to wake you, Mrs. Litzger-Gold, but could we chat about how we went through the Holocaust together?"

She'd have to wait until tomorrow. What she could do now, at least, was record everything she remembered. She went to boot up her computer. The printer caught her attention. Its power was off, but she never turned it off. Obviously someone else had been using her equipment without permission. Guess who?

She turned the printer on and its red malfunction light blinked—that was why Little Bit had shut it down. Nicole opened the printer. A tiny wad of paper was jammed in the rollers, preventing them from turning smoothly. She plucked it out with her tweezers and closed the cover. What Little Bit had been writing printed out.

THE DIARY OF ANNE FRANK

A BOOK REPORT BY ELIZABETH BURNS, GRADE 5
(Miss Nolan—this book report is for extra credit)

This book is a diary of a Jewish girl named Anne Frank who hid in an attic in Holland so that she wouldn't get caught by Nazis. She was there with her whole family. There were other people there too. She had a cat and kisses a boy named Peter. This was a very good book with a lot of emotions. But many people don't know that some very intelligent scholars think that Anne Frank did not really write this diary and it is a big fake.

Nicole was enraged. How could her sister write this drivel? But she knew how. Little Bit had been right there when she'd chatted online with Dr. Butthole Bridgeman, too ignorant to refute a word he'd said. She felt like putting her fist through a wall. Better yet, through Bridgeman's face. In a blind fury, she hurled her math book at the wall, cursing at the top of her lungs.

"Nicole, sweetie, are you all right?" Her mother hurried into her room, her father close behind.

Nicole sat on her bed, gingerly rubbing her foot. "I'm fine," she fibbed. "I stubbed my toe."

"It's not your head?" her mother probed, tipping Nicole's face to hers. "No pain, nausea, double vision—"

"No. I'm fine, Mom. Really." Suddenly she felt galvanized, and jumped to her feet. "I have to talk to Little Bit—"

"She's not here." Her mother still looked concerned. "She's sleeping over at Britnee's."

Nicole sank heavily onto her bed again. She couldn't tell Little Bit the truth until tomorrow. It was maddening.

"Are you sure your head doesn't hurt in any way?" her father asked. "Because your behavior is very erratic, Nicole."

"Maybe I'm just weird."

"Are you on drugs?" her father asked sharply.

"No, Dad, drug-free." She held up Anne Frank's diary. "In fact, I'm the only girl in the neighborhood doing homework on a Saturday night. You should be proud."

After five more minutes of parental quizzing on the state of her head and mental health, they left. Nicole stared at Anne's photo on the book cover for a while. Then she reopened the diary and started to read it again, from the beginning.

CAUTION!!! WEBSITE UNDER CONSTRUCTION!!!

Day 5, 2:56 a.m.

Frightening Thought du Jour: Time ticks away. Days, years, entire lifetimes. Amazing things happen to people. Then they die. If no one remembers their stories, the memory of who they were and what they did blurs, like watercolor paintings left in the rain. Until, finally, nothing is left on the canvas.

People Who Suck:
   a. Chrissy Hair-Toss Gullet
   b. Dr. Martin Bridgeman at the Center for the Scientific Study of Bull. Denier of the truth. Memory stealer. Thief. Liar.

People Who Don't Suck but We Never Tell Each Other the Truth:
   a. My mother: Sweet and clueless.
   b. My father: Judgmental and clueless.
   c. My sister: Future prom queen and clueless.
   d. Me: So clueless I didn't know I was clueless. So now I ask myself, "Girl X, just who is it you want to be?"

000001 MAGIC COUNTER

267

thirty-nine

Nicole awakened to birds singing. The clock read 7:45, which meant she'd slept less than five hours, yet felt as energized as if she'd slept for ten. She showered, pulled on some jeans and a flannel shirt, and tore out the phone book page with Paulette's number and address.

Her father was at the kitchen table, reading the newspaper and sipping coffee, when Nicole walked in. "My eldest is up before ten on a Sunday morning? What's the occasion?"

"None." As if she could even begin to explain. Nicole poured herself some coffee and checked the time again. Eight-thirty. She planned to call Paulette at nine. How slowly time passed when you wanted it to speed up; how quickly it fled when you wanted it to linger.

She could already imagine her fingers pushing Paulette's number into the phone, imagine the miracle of their conversation. Yes, she'd say, I understand now about things unspoken, things only the heart knows.

"Dad," she began, sitting across from him. "Did you ever read Anne Frank's diary?"

He was momentarily taken aback. "I'm sure I must have. Years ago."

"Meaning you don't remember? How could you not remember?"

He put the paper down. "Is this an interrogation?"

She stirred sugar into her coffee. "Maybe. You interrogate me about school all the time."

"What has gotten into you, Nicole?"

She had no idea. But she did know this: She felt reckless and brave enough to say things she usually only thought.

"I've just been thinking, Dad. We don't ever talk to each other. Not really."

"That is entirely untrue. We spend more time together than any other family I know."

"That's not what I mean." She had to make him understand. "Dad, you don't even know who I—" She paled. Her eyes had caught a small teaser at the bottom of the front page of the Sunday newspaper.

LOCAL HOLOCAUST SURVIVOR
LITZGER-GOLD, 74, DEAD. P. F-12.

"What is it, Nicole?"

Nicole rifled through the sections on the table, searching frantically for section F. "She can't be dead."

"Someone you know died?" her father asked gently.

"It just can't be." Nicole found the obituaries. There was a small photo of Paulette and an article about her. She had died the day before of a heart attack. The funeral was set for ten o'clock this morning at Congregation Beth El. Nicole noted the address. It was on the other side of town. She'd have to take two buses to get there. She lurched up from her seat, looking around for her backpack. "I have to go."

"Where?" her father asked, bewildered. She spotted her backpack in the corner and grabbed it. "Nicole," he repeated, "where are you going?"

"To see my friend."

forty

Nicole stood outside Congregation Beth El and watched several conservatively well-dressed latecomers scurry inside. She glanced down at her jeans and flannel shirt—maybe they wouldn't even let her in dressed like that. Maybe it didn't even matter. Paulette's body was in there, but Paulette wasn't.

Unbidden, the lyrics to a retro song her mother always sang when she was doing the bills filled Nicole's head, a song Nicole didn't even like. Something like, "Regrets, I've had a few, but then again, too few to mention."

Funny. She had almost too many regrets to mention: not listening when Paulette spoke, missing the chance to tell Paulette that she finally understood about things the heart knows, about their connection. Paulette had helped Claire escape from the Vel. She'd tried to save Nicole's life at Birkenau. But Nicole would never get to thank her. She'd have to carry her regrets around forever, because the only person who could ease her burden was now dead.

A man in a rumpled suit started to close the synagogue doors. Impulsively, Nicole hurried past his surprised face into the building. The main hallway was flanked by recessed windows and office doors. Beyond that was a circular foyer and the rear doors to the sanctuary.

She went in and stood in the back. The ceiling soared to a great height, inlaid with stained glass streaked by the sun. Near the front wall, above the raised stage, hung a burning orange light. Paulette's closed casket was on a stand below the stage. It was unpainted pinewood—plain and stark.

The seats of the synagogue were filled by hundreds of people. Nicole recognized Ms. Zooms in the crowd, even from the back. Everyone listened intently as a man spoke at the podium. He looked to be about the age of Nicole's parents.

"I can't remember exactly how old I was when my mother first told me about what had happened to her," he was saying. "She was a Jewish girl born and raised in Paris, a teenager during the Occupation. She lived a most extraordinary life. There is too much to tell, so the family has gathered some artifacts from her life for you to see and contemplate. They are displayed in a case in the social hall.

"Maman told me so many stories from the war years. Many of them were tragic, to be sure, but she would want you to remember her for so much more than that. She was very beautiful, and, by her own admission, quite a flirt. I remember her recounting how she had been madly in love with a Gentile boy named Charles. Because Jews were forbidden to attend movies, she used to cover her yellow star with her book bag so that she could sneak into the cinema with him. She was most afraid of getting caught not by the Nazis, but by her very strict mother."

Sad chuckles rippled through the sanctuary.

"She also used to tell me that when things got very bad, when she was the most scared and wanted to give up, some little thing would come along to give her hope again. Signs, she called them."

Nicole spoke to Paulette in her mind. *You have a nice son, Paulette.*

"And now," the man continued, "if you would permit me, I would like to share with you what my mother called her proof that she had defeated Hitler."

He nodded to some people in the first row, who joined him on the stage. "This is my wife, Shira." He put his arm around a woman with dark hair. "And these are our children, Paulette's grandchildren and her legacy. Benjamin, who is fourteen, Jacob, who is twelve, and Sarah, who is nine."

An ache welled up in Nicole's throat. People were crying loudly, but she would not let her own tears come. She wanted to be strong, because a long, long time ago, Paulette had been so strong for her.

Sarah has your golden hair, Paulette.

As the rabbi stood to hug each of Paulette's grand-children, Nicole slipped out of the sanctuary. She had the strongest urge to be alone with Paulette's things before the crowd of mourners came to look at them. She had just found a sign that pointed to the social hall when a surprised voice called to her.

"Nicole?"

She turned around. David. He wore a dark suit and tie. "What are you doing here?"

Nicole laughed. He was looking at her as if she'd lost her mind. How could she possibly explain that, in fact, she'd finally found it?

"What are you doing here?" she countered.

"My family belongs to this synagogue. Seriously, you didn't come for Mrs. Litzger-Gold's funeral, did you? You had zero interest in her."

"People change. Or maybe they find who they used to be. Like the me you knew in sixth grade."

He smiled. "I liked her."

"I liked her, too. See you around." She waited for him to enter the sanctuary before she opened the doors of the social hall.

Nicole saw it immediately. Resting on an easel just inside the entrance was a blown-up photo of Paulette Litzger as a teenage girl in Paris. She had short, dark hair, and wore wire-rim glasses; an entirely different face from the girl with the golden hair at the Vel d'Hiv and Birkenau.

She was another Paulette.

Nicole sagged against the closed door, no bones to hold herself upright, no blood coursing through her veins. It had all been a fantasy. There was no such thing as "signs." The heart was just a stupid muscle that pumped away until it quit forever; it didn't know anything at all. She hated that Zooms was right. There had been no Nicole Bernhardt. She hadn't met Anne Frank on a transport from Westerbork. And she had never known Paulette Litzger-Gold. Her only real connection to Paulette had been as a student who had only half-listened in Ms. Zooms' English class. Which was really no connection at all.

Nicole heard a male voice chanting a somber melody from the sanctuary; the funeral service must be nearly over. But she felt numb, unable to contemplate the walk back to the bus stop. So she made her way to the long glass case in which Paulette's things were displayed. A few handwritten words on a file card identified each object.

There was a photo. Caption: *Paulette and Sam on their twentieth wedding anniversary at Niagara Falls. Sam died in 1985.*

Another photo, older, in a brown leather frame. Caption: *The Litzger family in their Paris apartment—Paulette, her older brother, and her parents.*

Nicole saw that the mother was tall and slender, with the same eyes as Paulette. No resemblance at all to the mother in the Vel.

Next to the family photo was Paulette's girlhood French identity card, stamped Juive. *Juive is French for Jew.*

A set of United States citizenship papers. Caption: *Paulette considered the day of her citizenship one of the proudest days of her life.*

A letter signed by Steven Spielberg. *Paulette was invited to videotape testimony for the Survivors of the Shoah Visual History Foundation.*

A videotape. *Paulette's testimony for the foundation.*

Nicole was about to leave when the room darkened slightly as the sun ducked behind a cloud. She saw there were a few more items in the case that had been hidden by the sun's glare. She went to see what they were.

A spoon. *Paulette's spoon from Auschwitz-Birkenau.*

Next to the spoon Nicole saw a torn and much-folded scrap of paper, yellowed with age, with French handwriting too small and faded to make out until she pressed her nose against the glass.

NOTES DE JEUNE FILLE X

le 10 septembre 1943

Au peuple de Paris,

    Cher lecteur, si vous parcourez ce document et n'êtes pas un collabo-idiot, merci de le glisser sous la porte de quelqu'un qui le soit. Merci.

Salut Collabo Idiot! Je suis une jeune fille juive à qui les parents interdisent de sortir de la maison. Mais vous ne pourrez pas me réduire au sil—

276

Next to it, a translation:

NOTES FROM GIRL X

10 September 1943

To the people of Paris,

Dear reader, if you are reading this and are not a collabo idiot, please put this under the door of someone who is. Thank you.

Hello, Collabo Idiot! I am a Jewish girl forbidden now by my parents to leave our home, but still you cannot si(lence)—

Next to the translation, a file card: *This is the fragment of a letter that Paulette found on a Paris park bench in 1943; it gave her such hope that she made many copies and left them on other benches for people to find while keeping the original on her person until the moment of her death.*

Nicole felt herself lifted skyward by a shimmering golden light. For she knew without a doubt that she was reading her own handwriting. In French. She was Girl X. And somehow Paulette had found at least one of the notes that Mimi had smuggled out onto the streets of Paris.

No, Paulette Litzger-Gold had not been the Paulette who had tried to save her life at Birkenau. Instead, she was a different Paulette, one who had known Nicole by her writing

277

alone, and Nicole had helped to save hers. It had all happened. She really had been there. And with that knowledge, she left behind the earthbound girl who had believed she would always revolve around someone else. She was free.

CAUTION!!! WEBSITE UNDER CONSTRUCTION!!!

Day 6, 8:36 p.m.

The magic counter on the Girl X website still stands at 000001. If you are reading this now, you are 000002 or above. If you care enough to e-mail me, I can explain anything you're about to read that doesn't make sense, such as:

    a. why I went to Paulette Litzger-Gold's funeral;

    b. why I wrote down what happened afterwards; and

    c. why you should care.

One more thing. My name is Nicole.

The bus ride home from Paulette's funeral took forever. I found my mom in the kitchen unpacking groceries while she talked business on her cell phone. All I cared about was finding my little sister. I found her standing in front of my mirror, modeling my favorite sweater and my new earrings.

"I was only borrowing them," she said quickly. "You don't even take care of your stuff, anyway."

I sat on my bed. "You want 'em?"

She was beyond stunned. "What?"

On second thought, I really loved that sweater. "You can keep the earrings." I held out my hands for the sweater, and she gave it to me.

"You're actually *giving* me your new earrings? Why would you do that? You hate me."

"I don't hate you."

Little Bit folded her arms. "There has to be a catch."

"There is."

"I knew it."

"Little Bit, tell me one thing you want from me more than anything else in the world. I'll do it and throw the earrings in for free, if you do one thing for me."

"What?"

"Come somewhere with me for a couple of hours."

Little Bit looked skeptical. "That's it? That's all?"

"That's all. Name the one thing you most want from me."

Little Bit bit her lip. "You can't laugh. Promise."

"I promise."

"What I want is for you to call me Elizabeth."

How could I not have realized it meant so much to her? "Elizabeth," I said. "All right, Elizabeth. Let's go."

A half-hour later, Elizabeth stared out the window as our bus stopped at a light. "How much farther, Nicole?"

"A little ways."

"Why won't you tell me where we're going?"

Instead of answering, I said, " 'I never utter my real feelings about anything.' "

Elizabeth looked confused. "You don't?"

" 'My lighter, superficial side will always be too quick for the deeper side of me, and that's why it always wins.' "

Elizabeth made a face. "You are acting very weird and I don't understand what you're saying."

"I didn't say it. A friend did. I was quoting her."

"Quoting who?"

" 'That's the difficulty in these times: Ideals, dreams, and cherished hopes rise within us, only to meet the horrible truth and be shattered,' " I quoted again.

"Your friend said that?" Elizabeth looked thoughtful.

"There's more. Actually, she didn't say it, she wrote it. It's from her diary." I pulled Elizabeth's book report on Anne Frank's diary out of my pocket.

She looked embarrassed. "I didn't really read the whole thing," she admitted. "Are you mad I used your computer?"

"No. But I'm mad about what you wrote in this book report, when you didn't know what you were talking about."

"But that expert guy on the Internet said—"

"Anyone can call themselves an expert, Elizabeth. He's a liar. Anne Frank wrote every word of her diary. When we get back home, I'll show you the real proof."

"Okay."

I put my arm around her, Burb Girl in Training, currently hurtling down the highway toward Heatherville or Chrissyland or someplace I did not want her to end up. But maybe she could go a different way, end up someplace else entirely, if only I cared enough to try to show her how.

Ideals, dreams, and cherished hopes rise within us, only to meet the horrible truth and be shattered.

Maybe not shattered. I turned to my sister. "This is important, Elizabeth. We could have been in the Holocaust. You and me. Anne Frank could have been a friend of ours. Do you understand that?"

She looked up at me, her face more solemn than I had ever seen it before. And she nodded.

I nodded back. "Before we get to the exhibit, I'll tell you a little about Anne, okay? How she became a famous writer, and broke a million hearts."

TIME LINE OF ACTUAL EVENTS

Many historical facts and real figures from the past are woven into this work of fiction. The authors have taken care to reflect that history as accurately as possible while bringing Nicole's journey to life.

1929

12 **June** · Anne Frank born, Frankfurt, Germany

1933

30 **January** · Adolf Hitler appointed chancellor of Germany

 5 **December** · Anne Frank's family moves to Amsterdam, Holland

1934

19 **August** · 90 percent of German voters approve dictatorial powers for Hitler

1935

15 **September** · German Nuremberg race laws against Jews decreed

1938

12 **March** · German troops enter Austria

24 **April** · Germany orders all Jews to register wealth and property

23 **July** · All German Jews over the age of fifteen must have identity cards

9-10 **November** · Kristallnacht (Night of the Broken Glass) Mobs attack synagogues and Jewish businesses across Germany

1939

15 **March** · German troops seize Czechoslovakia (now Czech Republic and Slovakia)

 1 **September** · Germany invades Poland

 3 **September** · France and Great Britain both declare war on Germany; United States stays neutral

1940

10 **May** · Germany invades Holland, Luxembourg, and Belgium

12 **May** · Germany invades France

14 **June** · Paris occupied by German troops

18 **June** · Hitler tours Occupied Paris. Charles de Gaulle gives BBC radio
  address calling for continued resistance against the Nazis

22 **June** · German-French armistice signed. A portion of southern France
  remains under nominal French control with seat of government at Vichy

  October · French Statut des Juifs, a wide array of anti-Jewish laws, goes into effect

1941

16 **May** · Marshal Pétain approves collaboration with Nazis

22 **June** · Germany breaks treaty with Russia and invades that nation

22 **July** · French law permits confiscation of Jewish property

10 **September** · Nazi posters go up in Paris threatening that 50–100 French
  hostages will be shot for every German soldier killed by the Resistance

7 **December** · Japan attacks United States naval base at Pearl Harbor, Hawaii.
  United States declares war on Japan on 8 December

11 **December** · Germany declares war on United States; United States
  responds with declaration of war on Germany

1942

20 **January** · Decision for total extermination of Europe's Jews made at
  Wannsee Conference in Germany

27 **March** · First deportation leaves Drancy for Auschwitz, dozens follow
  through July 1944

7 **June** · Yellow star regulation goes into effect in Paris

6 **July** · Anne Frank and her family go into hiding at 263 Prinsengracht,
  Amsterdam, the Secret Annex

16–17 July · Vélodrome d'Hiver roundup of more than 12,000 foreign Jews in Paris

11 November · German troops occupy all of France in response to Allied invasion of North Africa

1943

31 January · French fascist militias, including the Permilleux Service, created
February · STO goes into effect, drafting French men to work in Germany
2 July · Alois Brunner assumes administration of Drancy detention camp

1944

6 June · D-Day, Allies invade Europe at Normandy, France

10 June · Oradour-sur-Glane massacre, 642 people murdered by Nazi SS

12 June · Anne Frank turns fifteen years old

31 July · Final official transport from Drancy

4 August · Anne Frank and family arrested in the Secret Annex

9 August · German army begins to withdraw from Paris

17 August · Brunner deports fifty-one prisoners from Drancy to Buchenwald in one final railway car attached to a German troop train, including Armand Kohn, chief administrator of the Rothschild Hospital, and his family. Escapees from this transport include Philippe and Rose-Marie Kohn

18 August · 1,500 prisoners at Drancy liberated by Allied troops

23 August · Paris liberated by American, British, Canadian, and Free French troops
September · Armand Kohn's youngest son, Georges-André Kohn, twelve, transferred to Auschwitz

3 September · Anne Frank and family deported from Westerbork to Auschwitz-Birkenau

5 **September** · Anne and family arrive at Auschwitz-Birkenau

28 **October** · Anne and her sister, Margot, are transferred to Bergen-Belsen concentration camp in northern Germany

12 **November** · Georges-André Kohn transferred to Neuengamme camp, near Hamburg, Germany, to be used in horrific medical experiments, including being injected with tuberculosis

1945

6 **January** · Edith Frank, Anne's mother, dies of starvation at Auschwitz

27 **January** · Auschwitz is liberated by Russian troops. Otto Frank survives

March · Margot and Anne Frank both die of typhus in Bergen-Belsen. (Peter Van Pels died at Mauthausen concentration camp.)

20 **April** · With British troops no more than three miles away, Georges-André Kohn and the twenty other children at Neuengamme are murdered by injection of fatal doses of morphine

8 **May** · V-E Day, Nazi Germany surrenders unconditionally to the Allies

1947 · First edition of Anne Frank's diary published by Otto Frank in Holland

1985 · Netherlands State Institute for War Documentation completes extensive scientific study authenticating Anne Frank's diary

1988 · Alois Brunner, commandant of Drancy camp, confirmed alive in Syria

1995–Present · Holocaust denial web sites proliferate on Internet

The total number of Jews murdered by the Nazis and their collaborators is estimated at no less than 5.2 million and as many as 6 million, representing two-thirds of all Jews alive in Europe at the beginning of the war. Of the approximately 300,000 Jews on French soil at the outbreak of the war, 76,000 were murdered.

FURTHER TIME LINE SOURCES:

britannica.com

uen.org

thehistoryplace.com

The Simon Wiesenthal Center

Bryce-Jones, Robert. *Paris Under the Occupation.* New York: Holt Rinehart and
   Winston, 1981.

Dank, Milton. *The French Against the French.* New York: Lippencott, 1974.

Josephs, Jeremy. *Swastika Over Paris.* New York: Arcade Publishing, 1989.

Klarsfeld, Serge. *French Children of the Holocaust: A Memorial.* New York:
   New York University Press, 1996.

Klarsfeld, Serge. *Le Memorial de la Déportation des Juifs de France.* Paris:
   Klarsfeld, 1978.

Muller, Melissa. *Anne Frank: The Biography.* New York: Henry Holt, 1998.

Rozett, Robert. *Encyclopedia of the Holocaust,* vol. 2. Edited by Israel Gutman.
   New York: Macmillan, 1989.

Weisberg, Richard H., and Michael R. Marrus. *Vichy France and the Jews.*
   New York: New York University Press, 1996.

ABOUT THE AUTHORS

With husband JEFF GOTTESFELD as dramaturge, CHERIE BENNETT has emerged as one of the nation's leading playwrights for young audiences—a two-time Kennedy Center New Visions/New Voices winner, for *Searching for David's Heart* (1998) and *Cyra and Rocky* (DRAMATIC, 1996), and three-time IUPUI/Bonderman certificate of award winner, once for *Anne Frank and Me* (DRAMATIC, 1997). Following that play's hit Off–Broadway run and dozens of other productions, Cherie and Jeff have finally adapted it to fiction.

Other recent work includes Cherie's *Life in the Fat Lane* (DELACORTE, 1998), an ALA Best Book for Young Adults, *Zink* (DRAMATIC, 1998, DELACORTE, 1999), and her popular Copley News Service syndicated teen column, "Hey, Cherie!"

Residents of Los Angeles and Nashville, they write for television and screen. Jeff is also a produced country songwriter. Their papers are being archived in the Child Drama Collection of the Hayden Library at Arizona State University. They can be reached at AuthorChik@aol.com.